**THE WALKING HILLS**

Zulus—that's what they called them, the ragged men and women who came to the Walking Hills for free land promised by the railroad. But the cattlemen had other ideas. They figured the land was theirs, and they weren't aiming to give it up. It wasn't long before there was a killing. And then another… and another…

Jeff Temple had traded in his scalpel for a gun, but he didn't want any part of this fight—not till Hammond showed him he had no choice. And it wasn't till they got to Doc that he saw what the real fight was about…

# THE WALKING HILLS

## Cliff Farrell

First published 1962 by
Doubleday & Company Inc
First British edition by
Ward Lock, Ltd, 1963

This hardback edition 1997
by Chivers Press
by arrangement with
Golden West Literary Agency

Copyright © 1962 by Cliff Farrell
Copyright © 1963 by Cliff Farrell in the British
Commonwealth
Copyright © renewed 1990 by Mildred Farrell
All rights reserved

ISBN 0 7451 8711 0

**British Library Cataloguing in Publication Data available**

Printed and bound in Great Britain by
Redwood Books, Trowbridge, Wiltshire

CENTRAL ARKANSAS LIBRARY SYSTEM
JACKSONVILLE BRANCH
JACKSONVILLE, ARKANSAS

# CHAPTER ONE

The afternoon was waning when Jeff Temple left the office of the Wardrum jail where he had visited his friend, Ramon Montez. They had talked for only five minutes although Jeff had come a long distance for that purpose. With them, five minutes had always been more than enough to reach an understanding.

He stood on the sidewalk, rolled a cigaret and lighted it. The breeze was warm but it carried the sleepy promise of fall, for the frosts came early in these northern plains. The Walking Hills to the south wore the blue haze of Indian summer.

The wind brought the fragrance of mown hayfields along Wardrum Creek on the fringe of town. It brought the sweetness of the sage. Beyond the hayfields lay miles of country. Sage and rabbit brush, buffalo grass and bunch. Swales and buttes and outcrops of weatherworn rock. The rabbit brush was in bloom, painting the land with a golden glow. It was a mighty country, a free land. And Ramon Montez might never see it again.

Jeff saw that Lish Carter, the sheriff, was watching him through the office window. He turned and walked away. The sheriff came to the door and stood there. Other eyes followed him as he moved down the street. He was accustomed to that. But he had never wanted it to be that way in Wardrum.

He walked westward along DeSmet Street, a straight, lithe, dark-haired man of thirty, quietly garbed in a dark sack suit. His hat and boots were of range origin. There was about him an air of discipline, that of a man who had set his course. A thin scar showed on his left jawbone, another on his chin.

Visible beneath the skirt of his coat was a black leather holster, weighted with a six-shooter. The holster fitted close against his thigh. It was to this that the eyes of the onlookers were attracted.

He walked into a section of town that was more familiar to him. This was old Wardrum, but even here, some of the landmarks were gone. Back of him, new town had grown up along the railroad tracks. The railroad was new too, having built into the country within the year. It was called the Canada & Mexico Overland and it had brought a boom to the country.

Beyond the railroad tracks the smoke of cookfires hazed the sky along Wardrum Creek, which was shrunken now to its late summer trickle. That was where the "Zulus" were camped, waiting to move into the Walking Hills when the railroad got its land grant and the range was opened to entry.

It was the railroad men who had pinned that name on the settlers. It had started back in the days when the Santa Fe was building through Kansas, and it still clung. The word was easy to scrawl in chalk on the weathered doors of boxcars in which the Canada & Mexico brought them in along with what belongings and livestock they owned.

The livestock usually consisted of a chicken or two, or a pig, so that the Zulus could get by under the railroad rules that permitted humans to travel in freight cars to care for dumb creatures.

Jeff turned off DeSmet Street at a corner so familiar to him there never would be any forgetting. Alex Crabtree's house stood a short distance down this side street.

Box elders shaded the rambling structure. Morning-glory vines climbed the porch, and a few purple blossoms still survived. A bony cowhorse was tethered to the iron hitchrail in front of the gate.

A small sign stood on the small lawn, surrounded by a bed of flowers. Jeff read the gilt letters.

ALEXANDER CRABTREE, M.D.

Jeff felt a knife-stab of regret. He told himself it had been a mistake to come here. What good were explanations now?

Through the open screen door he could see into the anteroom of Alex's office. Two patients were sitting in the worn leather chairs, waiting to see the doctor. One was a worried young mother with a fretting baby in her arms. She wore a sunbonnet and a thin, faded calico dress. Jeff decided that she was from the Zulu camp.

The other patient was a shaggy oldster who had a cane at his side and one ankle in a cast. He was a cowman by his garb, and belonged no doubt to the saddle animal at the rail. He sat stiffly facing the young mother, and it seemed to Jeff there was hostility between them.

The baby, Jeff decided, was probably colicky from heat and dust and the wrong diet, but it was suffering mainly from an inexperienced mother's worry and fussing.

He mentally offered his prescription to take care of his diagnosis: for the mother a little scoffing at her fears, a lecture on how tough and durable babies really are; for the baby a harmless sugar pill, with a hint of magical qualities for the mother's benefit. That would soothe the mother and at least do the infant no harm. A diet of goat's milk might be the answer to the colic.

Hettie Crabtree, the doctor's spinster sister, who served as his housekeeper and assistant, appeared from the inner office and beckoned. The young mother arose and followed her into the medical shop.

She came out after ten minutes. She was happier. She was even smiling. The baby had quieted and was investigating some tasty object in its mouth. Sugar pill, Jeff decided.

"Now where in the world can I get goat's milk in this country, Mis' Crabtree?" the mother was asking.

Hettie patted her on the shoulder. "I'll see to it," she said. "The Snyders keep goats for their young ones. They live on the edge of town. I'll go right over there and have them send one of their boys with it. Where will you be, young lady? At the Zu—the settler's camp, isn't it?"

The young woman bridled. "Yes," she said. "I'm what some people around here call a Zulu."

Jeff stood aside, lifting his hat, as the young mother hurried past him and headed up the street, carrying the quieted infant. He grinned a little, aware of a small inner glow of self-satisfaction.

His diagnosis had coincided with that of Alex's. Also the prescription. Doctoring included a little fakery, mumbo jumbo and mind reading. Also considerable praying. Instilling confidence in the patient often worked more miracles than drugs or the scalpel. Alex would refer to it as pouring some sand into their dad-burned craws. In this instance the sugar pill had been the sand, and the mother had been the real patient.

A sting of resentment drove through Jeff. He hadn't wanted to be carried into this line of thought. He was through with all of that sort of thing.

The cowman had his session in the inner office. It was short and he emerged grumbling. He came stumping angrily to the sidewalk on his cane and plaster-encased foot.

"Fifty cents fer tellin' me to scratch when the blasted cast itches!" he raged, addressing Jeff. "Ol' Doc Crabb must think money grows on tumbleweeds."

He thrust his cane in his belt, pulled himself in the saddle and rode away, one foot in a stirrup, still fuming.

Hettie began pushing chairs in place in the anteroom, preparing to close up shop for the afternoon. Jeff entered the gate, mounted the steps to the porch and tapped on the screen door.

"Botheration!" Hettie exclaimed. She raised her voice. "Alex! Don't you get out of the house! Looks like we've got another one!"

Jeff opened the screen door and stepped in. Hettie stopped in her tracks. She uttered a little scream, her hands going to her face in wonder. She was a tall, angular spinster who always dressed in spotless, starched white when she was on duty. She kept her hair dyed a fiery shade of red, a bit of vanity that did not begin to match the warm generosity of her nature. She had a prominent nose and a nasal voice, and there never had been anyone who really knew her who wouldn't fight for her if the need came.

Jeff said, "Hello, Aunt Hettie." He moved across the room and kissed her. She began to weep a little and clung to him. "Jeff! Oh, Jeff! It's been so long!"

The door of the inner office opened. Jeff turned. He said quietly, "Hello, Alex."

Dr. Alexander Crabtree stood gazing at him. Old Doc Crabb, they called him in Wardrum. He had grown a little more sparse and rawboned, a little frostier of brow and temple. His tanned bald area had spread. He wore his ever-lasting gray linen office jacket with the black sleeve guards.

His gold-rimmed spectacles were pushed up above his forehead. Some men said he carried spectacles just so he could say that he hadn't seen things that he didn't want to know about. He didn't need the eyeglasses when he went hunting. He was one of the finest wingshots Jeff had ever seen in action.

"It's been quite a while, Jeff," Alex said.

There was no challenge in his voice, no reproof, no recrimination. Not even a question.

Hettie came out of her state of shock. "You—you scamp!" she sobbed.

Jeff kept an arm around her. "I didn't figure I'd grown ugly enough to scare people," he said.

She pushed him away. "You ain't worth a tear or a sob," she wept. "You know that, don't you."

"That's better," Jeff said. "Now you're being yourself."

"Breakin' our hearts, an' then just walkin' in the door like it was only this mornin' you went away."

Alex spoke sharply. "Let it ride, Hettie!"

Hettie looked helplessly from one to the other. She kissed Jeff and rumpled his hair. "I'm so glad!" she breathed. "So glad you're—you're alive."

She tried to dry her tears. Snatching up her handbag, she said, "I've got to see the Snyders about that goat's milk."

She paused in the door and added, "Your room's just about like it was. I'll make up the bed when I get back an' clear out the bureau for your things. You're stayin' here, of course. This is your home."

Jeff hesitated. "Of course," he said.

He and Alex stood in silence for a time after the screen door had slammed. Alex spoke. "She'd have given a pretty penny to have stayed and heard what you talked about. She thinks a lot of you, Jeff."

He added, "We can talk better in the shop."

Jeff followed him into the inner office. The familiar old office with its shelves crowded with bottles of medicines and packages of pills, its cases of surgical equipment, its library of medical books.

Some of the books were new. Alex had always kept abreast of advances in his profession and made journeys at times to eastern clinics to absorb new ideas.

"What's that gadget in the corner?" Jeff asked.

"Portable operating table," Alex said. "I can lug it with me in the buggy on calls. It's equipped with reflector lamps. Cost me three hundred an' ninety dollars, shipped from Cincinnati, Ohio. Worth every cent of it. I've had my fill, working on kitchen tables in ranch houses and soddies, with only an oil lamp or a candle for light. My eyes aren't getting any younger."

That exhausted the conversation for a space. Alex waited. Jeff wandered around the room. He opened a copy of

Virgil's works in Latin. He turned to the penned inscription on the flyleaf:

> *From an old rawhide medicine man to a greenhorn. May he never lose his patience even if he loses a patient.*
>
> OLD DOC CRABB

Alex spoke dryly. "You forgot to take it with you."

"Yes," Jeff said.

"Virgil keeps a man brushed up on his Latin. Comes in handy when you don't want your patient to know you're prescribing for consumption when he thinks all he's got is a cold."

"Are you still the only doctor in Wardrum?" Jeff asked.

"Heck no. The place has grown. There're three of us now. The other two boys are young, but good doctors."

Jeff said abruptly, "I just talked to Ramon."

Alex nodded. "I figured you had."

"He seems to be getting a rough shuffle," Jeff said. "He's accused of attempted murder of a Camo agent and of robbery of an express car. He says the stuff was planted on his place. He says he didn't shoot at that Camo agent. He only wanted to teach him a lesson. He notched on the horse."

Alex nodded. "Lucky for the agent. Ramon's a pretty good shot. He got the horse. But the Camo man got a busted leg out of it in the fall."

"Ramon never robbed that car," Jeff said. "His word is good with me. He never lied to me. Nor me to him."

"You two were mighty good tillicums," Alex nodded. "Never saw two men who seemed so different hit it off so good. Ramon wouldn't lie to you, and that's for sure. He owes you a lot. And Dolores too. They both know that. Things would have been a lot tougher on them when they first came into the Walking Hills if you hadn't taken them under your wing."

"What did these Camo agents have against him?"

Alex shrugged. "Maybe the charge they've got against him isn't what he's really being held for."

"You mean because he's an Argentino? Because he's different?"

"Maybe. Folks around here had about forgotten that he was from down there. I hadn't heard him called an Argentino in years until just lately when this trouble broke out.

I suppose it started again among these new people that keep flocking in. Why, dratburn it, I used to know every human being and their dogs and cats for a hundred miles in any direction. Now I feel like a stranger."

"You mean the Zulus? They don't really believe they can make a living farming the Walking Hills, do they?"

"They're willing to bet the government they can make out, provided Teddy Roosevelt signs to open the Hills."

"He hasn't signed it yet?" Jeff asked. "I thought it was all cut and dried."

"It was at first. The bill to charter a right-of-way for Camo through the range slid by in both houses on greased wheels. Then the ranchers woke up. A rider had been slipped into the bill which changed the Walking Hills from grazing reserve back to land for public entry. The Walking Hills Cattle Association reared up on its hind legs. Some of us went to Washington and talked to the President personally."

"You were one of them?"

"Me and Peter Mackay and Evans Johnson. The ranchers asked me to go. Teddy Roosevelt was real nice to us. He listened close and said he'd look into it. The bill's been on his desk ever since. Nobody knows what he's decided to do."

"Both sides will get a fair shake," Jeff said. "My father knew him well and admired him. They became friends back in the eighties when Dad went into the Black Hills in Dakota on a gold rush. Roosevelt was ranching in the Badlands at the time. They did a lot of hunting together."

Alex nodded. "Matt often talked about Teddy. They were another pair that seemed so different, but hit it off well. Teddy Roosevelt had planned on coming out here to the Hills for a hunting trip with your father just about the time Matt was killed."

"Too bad Roosevelt didn't make it," Jeff said. "If he'd seen the Hills he'd know how rough it can be on homesteaders down there. Don't they know the only water between here and the Grindstones is in Little Beaver and that there's mighty little of that?"

"Go down to the Zulu camp and try to tell 'em that," Alex said. "They'll likely ride you out of the place on a rail."

He paused, then said, "Or maybe they wouldn't get rough with you, Jeff. From what I hear, you don't let people push you around. You do the roughing."

Jeff let that pass without challenge. "Bill Hammond's in charge here, isn't he?"

Alex nodded. "He's general manager of Camo. They even named Hammond Street for him."

"What will Camo get out of this?"

"Usual land grant for new railroads, every other section. They're bringing in the Zulus to squat on railroad land as soon as Roosevelt signs the charter. The rest of the country will be filed on too by homesteaders."

"They don't know what they're doing." Jeff said.

"You can't talk to Zulus. All they can think of is that it's free land."

"What about Ramon?" Jeff asked. "I'm not the only friend he's got. You're one of them, Alex. I appreciate your letting me know he was in this fix."

Alex's brows lifted. "Me?"

"The telegram," Jeff explained. "It caught up with me at Spokane."

"I didn't send any telegram," Alex said.

Jeff eyed him. "Your name was signed to it."

"I didn't send it. Maybe I should have. Whoever sent it did the right thing even if he did forge my name. But why did he pick mine to use?"

"You know why," Jeff said.

Alex moved to a cabinet, poured glasses of brandy and handed one to Jeff. "Soothes the nerves," he said. He spun the brandy gently in the glass. "Yes, I know why," he said. "I still know you'd come if I asked you to, no matter how far away you were."

He added, "Whoever sent that message knows that too."

Silence again came between them for a space. "All right," Jeff said. "Ask me why I did it. Why I quit."

"You don't have to tell me anything, Jeff."

"You're the only person I *do* have to explain it to. The only one who'd understand."

"What if I didn't understand?"

"I found out I wasn't cut out to be a doctor," Jeff said.

Alex shook his head. "Wrong. You had the flame."

"Flame? You're right. It burned me. I've still got the scars."

"Some men who call themselves doctors only know what's printed in books and what other men try to teach them. You were meant to be the other kind of a doctor, Jeff. You'd have taught others. You would have been a healer. It's inside you. This flame. And you would have been a fine surgeon. A rare combination. Instead, you . . ." Alex broke it off with a helpless gesture.

". . . Turned into a destroyer," Jeff said.

"I can't believe that," Alex said. "But you *are* wasting your life. God gave you the talent. It's sacrilege not to use it. You must have got it from your mother—this gift that the world ought to have from you. But you turned the other way. You decided to walk in your father's footsteps."

Jeff stiffened, an anger rushing up in him. Alex lifted a hand, silencing him. "Not that I'm saying anything against Matt Temple. He was my friend."

"But he was a destroyer too, not a doctor," Jeff said. "A killer."

Alex now also stood straight and angry. "Nobody ever called Matt Temple a killer. At least no one who really knew him. He was a fighting man, yes. A rough man if he came after you."

"But he killed three men," Jeff said.

"Yes. And took his own punishment. Twice, right in this room, I figured he was going to die from lead that men had shot into him. I got the bullets out of him and he lived. A town marshal in those days had to be tough."

"You saved him both of those times, Alex," Jeff said. "You are a healer too, and a good one. But the third time you lost."

Alex's face was gray, set. "Matt was dead when they carried him in," he said.

"And my mother?"

"I tried," Alex said. "But it wasn't any use."

"You couldn't save her," Jeff said. "But you did save the man who killed them. You pulled him through."

"Yes," Alex said grimly.

"He wasn't worth saving. Yet she died and he lived."

"That's been argued since the beginning of time," Alex said wearily. "I had to do it. You know that."

"Don't start throwing your Hippocratic oath at me," Jeff said. "I know it by heart. It was the one thing they taught me well."

"I'm a doctor, not a judge," Alex said. "He belonged to the law. I saved him so they could hang him."

"But they didn't hang him."

"That was up to the law. It was no longer in my hands."

Jeff nodded. "It was no longer in your hands. But it still doesn't square up. She was an angel. She's dead and he's alive. I understand he's here in Wardrum."

Alex abruptly set his glass aside. "My God, Jeff! That isn't why you came back? Not because of Red Kramer?"

"You mean, did I come back to kill him? No. I didn't even know he was here until Ramon told me a few minutes ago. I wouldn't know Kramer if I saw him. I've never laid eyes on him."

"Of course," Alex said. "I shouldn't have asked that."

"You've heard that I'm a killer," Jeff said.

Alex nodded. "Yes. I've heard that. But people have never dared say it in my hearing a second time. I know you too well."

"In my business, a reputation like that helps," Jeff said. "When people are afraid of you they're easier to handle. But, up to now, the only ones I've killed were on an operating table."

"Don't say that, Jeff. A doctor can only do his best."

"Do you remember me writing to you and Aunt Hettie about a girl I was interested in back in Ohio when I was finishing my surgical training at a Cincinnati hospital?"

Alex nodded. "Angelina Simmons, wasn't it? You seemed to be quite taken with her."

"Angie was nineteen. She was gay. She was witty. She liked people. We both did. We might have married some day. We were too busy enjoying life at the time to be that serious. I never told you why that never came about."

"You quit mentioning her in your letters," Alex said.

"She's dead," Jeff said. "She was killed less than a year after Mother and Dad were killed here in the Walking Hills."

"Killed?"

"A man went insane on the street and began shooting. He shot two passersby before the police blasted him down. Angie was one of them."

Alex started to speak but Jeff silenced him. "I've never talked about it to anyone. You're the only person I'll ever speak to about it. Angie was still alive when they brought her in. The hospital where I was finishing my training happened to be the nearest. All of the experienced surgeons were gone. I was there on duty alone. I couldn't save her. I tried. How I tried!"

"Keep talking, Jeff," Alex said. "It's best to drain this out of you."

"I was responsible," Jeff said. "I was the one who turned that man loose so that he could kill her."

"*You* turned him loose?"

"He had come to the hospital a few days before it happened. He complained of headaches and of times when he couldn't remember anything. He was an alcoholic. He was turned over to me, for it seemed like a commonplace case that an interne could handle. I gave him the usual pills and told him to eat more solid meals and to drink less. He seemed to think his complaint was more serious than that. But because I was one of those superior beings, a doctor, and also being a little miffed at having to bother with a case that I considered beneath my talents, I laughed at his fears and told him to come back in a few days."

Jeff again felt the agony of bitter memories. He finished the brandy. "Two days later Angie was dead on my operating table. Other doctors held a post-mortem on the man who killed her. He was suffering from a brain tumor. An operation might have saved him. Instead, he had gone criminally insane. I wasn't a superior being. I was a murderer."

"No!" Alex protested. "You can't say that. Is this why you . . .?"

"That's when I realized I was only mortal," Jeff said. "Or less. I came west. Jim Hill offered me a job with Great Northern. He had been a friend of my father's. Dad had worked as a special agent for Jim Hill when Great Northern was pushing rails across the plains to Spokane. I'm following right in his footsteps. I carry a gun as a special agent for the railroad. I keep order in boom camps and shoot trouble wherever it pops up. I'm on leave from G.N. for a few weeks right now."

"What a waste," Alex sighed. "What a frightful waste. I've had letters from men under whom you trained. Even some from Vienna. They all asked what had happened to you. All of them said you had a brilliant future, especially as a surgeon."

"They were wrong," Jeff said.

They stood listening to the shrill squeaking of an unoiled wheel as it came down the street. Jeff decided the sound came from a wheelbarrow that someone in a hurry was propelling. It halted at the gate of the house.

Footsteps sounded on the porch. "Doctor!" a girl's voice called. "Doc Crabb!"

"Somebody must have gone and got hurt," Alex said.

He hurried to the anteroom into which flooded an assortment of excited visitors. First came a girl wearing a riding habit, boots and a range hat that was held on her head by a chinstrap. With her was a barefoot boy of about ten in patched denim breeches and a gingham shirt.

Between them they carried the limp form of a liver-colored dog that lay sprawled on the top of a packing case that was being used as a litter. The animal, by the length of its ears, had considerable hound in its lineage.

Close at the heels of the litter-bearers came a calico-clad girl of about six who clutched the hand of a tow-headed boy of no more than four. Great tears were painting white streaks down the dusty faces of the smaller ones. The tow-head began wailing loudly.

"What'n blue tophet!" Alex gasped. "Lila, you can't—!"

"I want you to fix up this poor little dog," the girl said breathlessly. "I'm afraid its leg is broken."

## CHAPTER TWO

"Cussination!" Alex moaned. "Take that blasted animal to Gus Reimer's place. He does all the veterinary business."

That touched off a louder chorus of weeping on the part of the two small children.

"That old rumpot!" the girl said scornfully. "All he knows is how to blow pills down the gullets of sick horses. If this poor puppy's got a broken leg you've got to fix it, and that's that. It was my fault. My horse kicked him. I didn't act fast enough. I could have prevented it."

Alex eyed the dog with distaste. "Puppy?" he snorted. "He looks more like a yearling moose. If his leg's busted there's likely not much use—"

The girl silenced him with an angry glare and a motion toward the weeping children.

To Alex's horror she and the boy pushed past him and carried their burden into his inner office. Alex uttered a yell of protest, but he was unheeded. They tenderly slid the dog off the litter onto his operating table.

"I'll have to disinfect the whole dad-burned place!" Alex screeched. "That pothound's full of fleas."

"Who cares about a few fleas?" the girl sniffed. She lifted the small towhead in her arms, cuddling him and trying to stem his tears. She wasn't too successful. Jeff noted that a few tears were glistening on her own cheeks.

He saw now that she was no mere slip of a girl. She was, in fact, a very attractive female. She petted the dog, and the animal tried to thump its tail but subsided with a whimper of pain.

Alex, scowling and grumbling, ran his hands over the animal's injured leg. The canine patient uttered a protesting yelp and tried to struggle, but Alex soon won its confidence.

Alex's scowl deepened as he continued his examination. He looked at Jeff. "Busted, all right," he said. "But it's more like a green stick. Square in the middle of the forearm."

"Greenstick?" the girl echoed. "Forearm?"

It was Jeff who explained. "A greenstick fracture is medical lingo for a partial break and a bent bone. The forearm in a dog is the long bone in the front leg."

"Can you . . . ?" she asked, turning to Alex.

"Oh, I reckon," Alex said grumpily. "Being as he's no more'n a pup it'll likely mend in a hurry. Fifty dollars worth of trouble on a fifty-cent dog."

"I'll pay," the girl said.

Alex glared at her. "Who said anything about pay? I don't take pay for stealin' business away from Gus Reimer."

"I'll pay you, mister," the older boy spoke up. "As soon as I grow up an' can earn the money."

"Hah!" Alex snorted. "That's about how long I have to wait for most of my fees."

He prepared chloroform, laid out pine lengths to form into splints and got bandages and instruments ready.

Jeff took charge of the anaesthetic. "I'll handle this end of it," he said.

"Are you a doctor too?" the girl asked.

"No," Jeff said gruffly.

He stroked the dog's head, talking to it, and began using the chloroform.

"I forgot that you two don't know each other," Alex said. "Seems like you ought to. Lila, this is Jeff Temple. He grew up from a tadpole in this country. Jeff, Lila Mackay."

"Temple?" she repeated. "I've heard the name."

"Not lately," Alex said. "Jeff's pappy was town marshal here about the time you folks came into the Hills."

A shadow came into her face. "Of course. Matt Temple. We had just started getting well acquainted with your parents when they—they died."

She looked at the children, as though debating whether to continue. "My father is Peter Mackay," she said. "We ranch in the Walking Hills. The Rocking PM brand."

The older boy whirled and stared at her. He almost

forcibly snatched his small brother from her arms. "I might have knowed you was a Mackay!" he choked. His thin face was bitterly hostile.

"Wait a minute, sonny!" Alex exclaimed. "That's no way to act. Lila's only trying to help you."

"I'm thankin' her for what she's done for Prince," the boy said. "But we don't need no more help from her."

"What did you say your name was, darling?" Lila Mackay asked gently.

"Charles Slocum," the boy said grimly. "My parents call me Chub."

He turned to Alex. "Kin you make Prince well, mister? I told you I'd pay you for it as soon as I could."

"You're one of the settlers waiting for the opening, aren't you?" Alex asked.

The boy nodded. "My pop says the cattlemen aim to run us out of the country. He says the Mackays are the worst of the lot."

"That isn't true, Chub," Lila Mackay said. She suddenly seemed near to real tears. "As for the Mackays, there's only my father and me. But let's go in the other room while the doctor fixes Prince's leg."

Chub Slocum pulled away from her when she tried to take his arm. He drew his brother and sister closer. "I reckon we'll stay here with Prince," he said.

Alex nodded. "It's all right, Lila. Let them stay."

The dog lay limp under the effects of the choloroform Jeff was applying. Alex began working, using clamps. The children stood silent and awed, their eyes wide with apprehension.

Alex lifted his head, listening. The clatter of hooves and the grind of wheels arose. The sound came nearer and halted in the street. Bootheels pounded the porch and a hand banged the screen door.

"Doc!" an excited man called. "Doc! Are you there? The baby's comin'. My wife says this time it's for sure. Will you git a move on, fer God's sake."

Alex gave Jeff a resigned look. "I never saw a cussed baby yet that didn't want to born at the wrong time," he snorted. "And I haven't had my supper yet!"

He waited, eyeing Jeff challenging. Jeff hesitated, then finally shrugged. "All right," he said. "Get going."

He looked at Lila Mackay. "I'll do my best to finish splinting the pup. Maybe you could take over this hood and give Prince a whiff of the dope whenever I tell you to. I'll show you how it works."

"I'll try," she said.

Jeff began working on the dog. Alex got his medical bag, pulled on his coat, lighted a cigar and went stalking out of the house at the heels of the nervous expectant father.

"If this is another false alarm, Henry," Alex was saying, "I'll hand you a bill for the lost time anyway, dratburn it. This is the second time you've come in a lather when all your wife wanted was to talk to somebody. And she's a talker."

"Can't you walk a little faster, Doc!" the man implored.

"I've had more patients get well before I got there than I've saved by busting a gut to hurry," Alex growled.

The vehicle left at a gallop. Jeff formed pads and shaped splints. Everything in this room and in this task aroused memories that he had wanted to remain dead. It had been more than three years since he'd handled any type of surgical equipment. But the touch came back. And the memories.

The dog quivered and barked in its narcotized dreams. The children froze and quit breathing. Lila Mackay peered apprehensively at Jeff.

Jeff grinned and said, "You're doing fine. So's the patient. You can quit now. I'm just about finished."

She stood back, drawing a sigh, and went a little limp. Jeff looked around and found the smelling salts just where they had always stood, and thrust the bottle under her nose. She choked and rubbed her watering eyes until she recovered.

Jeff finished the final knot in the bandages that held the splints on the patient. He formed a muzzle of strips of the material and fitted it in place.

He slapped Chub on the back. He poked the small towhead in the ribs until he squirmed and giggled. He chucked the freckled little girl under the chin. "Let's have a few smiles for a change," he said.

"Will Prince be all right?" Chub Slocum asked shakily.

"He ought to be until he gets kicked by another cowpony, which will likely happen if he fools around them," Jeff said. "We'll have to keep him muzzled, or he'll chew off the splints the first chance he gets."

He found a dollar in his pocket and pushed it into the boy's pocket. "Buy a good strong leather muzzle, or have your dad make one," he said. "You can likely get one at

Cal Dayton's mercantile for about a quarter. Buy Prince a dime's worth of bologna, and Cal will likely give you a mess of liver for him. Just blow the rest of it in on candy and whatever suits your fancy for you and your pardners here."

The dog had revived. It began flopping its long legs, trying to get to its feet. Jeff petted it soothingly. The children burst into laughter as the animal peered, dumbfounded, at its bandaged leg.

"Don't give old Prince any more than a few laps of water tonight," Jeff said. "He might get sick. By morning he can drink all he wants. Make sure the muzzle stays on him. Keep him full of food so as to get his mind off chewing at the splints. If he does manage to get them off, take him to Dr. Crabtree right away for repairs."

Jeff carried the dog out of the house and placed it in the wheelbarrow. Chub trundled it away, the wheel screeching and the two smaller Slocums skipping happily alongside. Prince's head was hanging overside. He was still a very dizzy and abused hound.

Lila Mackay had remained on the porch, watching. Jeff re-entered the house and she followed him into the medical shop. He found rubber gloves and sprayed the table with carbolic solution and scrubbed it down. He took care of the equipment that had been used.

"Aunt Hettie would do this when she came back," he said. "But it's always best to be prepared. When people need a doctor they sometimes need him in a hurry."

"Yes," she said.

She had removed the wide-brimmed range hat that had shaded her face. He judged that she was about twenty-three. There was completion in her features—the full and quiet attractiveness of a young woman of character and refinement. Her hazel eyes were clear and frank. Her tawny hair just escaped being red. Her face was sensitive, with good cheekbones and cheeks so slender they were at the point of being thin.

"So you knew my parents," he said abruptly.

"Not closely," she said. "We hadn't been in the Walking Hills long enough to become well acquainted."

She added slowly, watching him. "You know, of course, that Red Kramer was working for us at Rocking PM at the time."

Jeff's eyes searched her face, trying to learn where this was leading. "No," he said. "I didn't know."

"He wasn't a regular rider," she said. "He had only been hired to help with the calf brand."

"I see," Jeff said.

"Dad didn't know Kramer was the kind of a man he—he was."

"And what kind of a man was he?"

"You're not making it easy for me," she said.

"It sounded like you were trying to get around to saying Kramer was a gun-slinger," Jeff said.

"If you want to put it that way—yes."

"And that's a word not to be used in polite company, I take it."

She stood taller, her chin lifting. "I'm only trying to tell you that our only responsibility was in giving him a job that kept him in the country. But it was a personal grudge that we didn't know about. Your father and Kramer had had trouble. Your father had arrested him a few days before all this happened, when Kramer was drunk and trying to start trouble in a saloon in town. Kramer resisted but your father hit him with his pistol and threw him in jail. Kramer paid a fine and was released the next day."

"Buffaloing is the word," Jeff said. "Knocking them out with the barrel of a six-shooter. Some call it roughing them up. Roughing them seems to be a Temple trademark."

"I didn't say that!" she exclaimed.

"It's better than killing them," Jeff said.

"In this case it wasn't. It was your parents who were killed."

"Kramer was turned loose."

"Two witnesses testified it was an accident," she said. She paused, then added, "Those two men were riding for my father at the time too. They were roundup hands he had put on at the same time he hired Kramer."

Jeff eyed her. She stood her ground. "They seemed to have no connection when they were hired," she said. "But they hung together afterward."

Jeff was wishing she hadn't brought it up. The loss of his father and mother still was hard to bear. He had been far away when it had happened, so far that it had seemed unreal—until now.

Matt and Nellie Temple had been riding in a spring wagon, heading for the Grindstone Mountains with a camping outfit for an elk hunting holiday. A shot from the brush had torn through Matt Temple's back. He had fallen from the wagon and the horse, running away, had capsized the vehicle, hurling Jeff's mother among boulders.

Matt Temple had clung to his pistol. When the man who had fired the shot appeared from the brush Matt Temple put a bullet in him. He was Red Kramer.

All three of the injured had been brought to town in wagons. Jeff's father died on the way. His mother died on the operating table in Alex's office. But Alex had saved the life of Red Kramer.

Kramer's lawyer produced two witnesses at the inquest who testified that they had been present at the time and that Kramer had been shooting at an antelope, not knowing that anyone was within range. For lack of contrary evidence the law finally had released Kramer.

"Why are you telling me all this?" Jeff asked.

"Because you didn't seem to know. My name, Mackay, didn't seem to mean anything to you when Doc Crabb introduced us."

"I haven't spent much time in Wardrum these past few years," Jeff said. "I was in Europe when my parents were killed. Word didn't reach me for weeks."

"Were you in Vienna?"

He nodded, and she said, "That's a mecca for medical students, isn't it? Famous clinics are there."

He didn't answer that. "If you're trying to find out if I came back here because of some vendetta against your father," he said, "you can rest easy. I didn't even know until today there was anyone in the Hills by the name of Mackay."

She suddenly extended a hand. "Thank you, Mr. Temple."

"For what?"

"Well, for one thing, for helping that poor dog. And for being so kind to those children."

"Aren't you supposed to be kind to children? Even to Zulu children?"

She winced. "That's a railroad man's name for those misguided people."

"It seemed to me that cattlemen are their demons and that Peter Mackay is the one with the biggest fork in his tail."

She abruptly picked up her hat and turned to leave. "My

father's no demon. He's kind and honest. But that doesn't mean he won't fight for his rights."

"You mean fight the Zulus?"

"Those people are being exploited, and you know it."

"Why should I know it?"

"I misled you a trifle," she said. "I *had* heard of you. Everyone in Wardrum has heard of Jeff Temple. You've made quite a reputation for yourself with Great Northern. Now you're home. Everyone knows why you're here."

"To help exploit the Zulus?"

"Frankly, yes. You know it's the truth. They're poor, bewildered people. They're being brought here by Camo, believing they'll find free land. All they'll find is misery and poverty. Or their graves."

"You mean that the cattlemen will run them out or kill them?"

The heat of her anger died. She gazed at him levelly. "You were raised in this country. You know what I mean. The Walking Hills will kill people like them, not the cattlemen."

She turned and walked out of the room. Jeff slid into his coat, picked up his gunbelt and followed her, buckling the belt into place. "I'll walk with you," he said. "Where are you bound?"

"I can make it alone," she said.

"I told you there was no feud," he said. "And between the two of us least of all."

She relented and he walked with her down the street. Dusk had come. The first crispness of the night was in the air. She carried her hat, swinging it by the strap. The breeze stirred her hair, bringing out new coppery hues.

"Do you know Ramon Montez?" Jeff asked.

"Of course," she said. "And his wife Dolores."

"Ramon happens to be a friend of mine."

She looked at him quickly. "Is that why you're here?"

Jeff nodded. "He's a real friend. We were tillicums. Up here that's what they call pardners who hit it off well. It's a Siwash word, I guess."

"I've learned the word," she said. "I was born in Texas, but I'm beginning to consider myself a native here. Ramon's in bad trouble. He's charged with trying to kill a Camo agent."

She paused, giving him a sidewise inspection, then added, "That places you in an awkward position, doesn't it?"

"Awkward?"

"You have a problem of loyalty. Which is it to be? Do you help Ramon, or do you stay with Camo?"

"You have things twisted. I'm working for Great Northern, not Camo."

"Railroads are your bread and butter. Or, in your case, it's probably cake and champagne. I imagine you're well paid in your line of work."

"What, exactly, is my line of work?"

She ignored that question. "You probably developed a taste for the better things of life when you were in Vienna."

"I lived real high," Jeff said. "In an attic. With the mice. We shared the cake and champagne. I often had as much as a dollar and a half, American, a week to blow in."

"Then why did you—?" she began. She decided against finishing the question.

They had entered DeSmet Street. It was Saturday night and old town had come to life. The cattlemen were pouring into town for their weekly round of shopping and conviviality. Saddlestock and vehicles lined the street. The stores were lighted and doing business.

"We're staying at the hotel," she said.

"You're in town for awhile?"

"Only overnight. It's a regular Saturday spree for me. I do the stores, then go to church on Sunday. I like to sing in the choir."

A powerfully-built man with graying hair and mustache, who had been impatiently pacing the plank platform of Cal Dayton's mercantile, came striding to meet them. He was a veteran cattleman by every item of garb and craggy, weathered feature. His bootheels had an authoritative, hammer-sound on the sidewalk.

"Lila, dammit!" he exclaimed. "I been huntin' even the gopher holes for you for an hour. Where'n blue hell have you been?"

"It was this way, Daddy," she said. "My horse kicked a dog and I took the poor critter to Doc Crabb. This gentleman here sort of patched up the pooch."

"How's that again?"

She laughed. "This is my father, Peter Mackay," she said to Jeff. "He's the demon you were talking about. Take a close look. You'll see the forked tail."

"What's this she's been tellin' you Mr.—Mr.—?" Mackay chuckled.

"Temple," she said before Jeff could answer. "Jeff Temple. He's the son of Matt Temple."

Peter Mackay's hand, which he had started to offer, halted. After a moment he lowered it.

"I see," he said. He drew into himself. He was wary and waiting for Jeff to make the next move. Jeff saw that Mackay had received word of his arrival. It seemed to be common knowledge in Wardrum; they seemed to know more about why he was here than he did himself.

Mackay's manner was obviously hostile. Jeff decided against making any denials. If they wanted to prejudge him, let them. He lifted his hat to Lila Mackay and said, "I'll be moving along. Good night, Miss Mackay. Good night, sir."

He could almost feel the hard impact of Peter Mackay's bleak eyes on his back as he walked away. He surmised that Lila would have questions to answer.

## CHAPTER THREE

Jeff walked westward through old town, leaving the stores and activity behind. The sidewalks ended and he took to the rutted, unpaved wagonroad that wound among the scattered outlying sodhouses and ragtag structures of early-day Wardrum.

People he had known from boyhood still lived here, no doubt. He wondered what sort of a welcome they would give him now if he appeared at their doors. He kept telling himself that it would be best for him if he left this place.

This was not the Wardrum of his boyhood. Life had seemed simple enough then. It had been a frontier cattle town. Rough. Sometimes violent. But friendly too. It had been a country of pioneers, of men and women who had fought for what little they possessed. They had fought the Sioux and the Shoshones. Above all, they had found the plains themselves. They had been mighty in their pride and had made their own law.

This Wardrum seemed to be an eddy of deep currents. Peter Mackay's refusal to shake hands with him had been a savage ripple, breaking to the surface.

The road carried him higher and he turned into the

little cemetery which stood on a rise overlooking the town. The lamps of Wardrum were glittering in the early darkness. Stars were spangling the sky. A switch engine was working in the Camo yards, its firebox sending occasional ruddy flashes across the town.

Beyond the railroad tracks the glow of campfires marked out the shacks and tents of the Zulu camp. A dance was being organized in the camp. Jeff could see the Zulus gathering there. A fiddle and a banjo struck up. A drum beat time.

Jeff found the grave where his parents were buried. He stood beside the headstone, his hat in his hand. The plot was neat and green with grass in contrast to the dry, weedy appearance of the majority of the resting places. He had sent money regularly to Willie Crane, the handy man of the town, for care of the graves.

This place brought regrets that were hard to endure. It brought a rage against the man who had fired the shot that had ended the sweetness of his mother's life, taken the strength of his father's existence.

"I'll be back," he said aloud. "I'll always come back as long as you two are here."

He left the cemetery and returned slowly into town. He was weighed down by the knowledge of futility, a lack of purpose. He had to admit it now. He was drifting.

He headed toward the settlers' camp, drawn by the sounds of the music and dancing. He crossed the Camo railroad tracks and stood in the shadow of a line of empty freight cars on the last siding, gazing from the elevation of the roadbed down into the camp in the flats along the creek. The settlement was bigger than he had anticipated. There were a few tents that seemed adequate, but for the most part the Zulus lived in half-dugouts or shacks improvised of packing cases and sheet iron.

The dancing was going on in the clearing where creek sand had been spread to afford a dustless underfooting. A square dance was in progress, with a caller's voice issuing bullfrog croaking above the music and shuffle of feet.

Jeff sighted Chub Slocum among the onlookers. The boy was with his brother and sister and they stood beside a man and woman who were obviously their parents. The woman held a small baby in her arms.

Jeff grinned. Even the hound with the broken leg had been brought with them. The animal lay enthroned in the wheelbarrow on a bed of dry grass.

Jeff became aware that he was not the only spectator from this dark viewpoint. Half a dozen men were standing silently a short distance down the line of sidetracked cars. The light of the campfires reached them faintly. They were cattlemen by their garb. They watched the camp in silence for a few minutes longer, evidently talking among themselves.

Then they left, walking around the far end of the string of cars and heading off across the tracks toward town, the crunch of their boots receding in the gravel. Jeff had identified one of them. Peter Mackay.

Jeff walked into the camp and moved among the bystanders until he reached the Slocum family. "Howdy, Chub," he said. "How's Prince feeling by this time?"

Chub was pleased and flattered. "He's just fine," he stammered. "I only gave him a few swallers o' water, like you told me to. An' Dad made him a leather muzzle."

"I'm Jeff Temple," Jeff said to the couple. "You're Chub's parents, I take it."

"This is the man I told you about what fixed Prince's leg, Paw," Chub explained.

The man extended a hand. "I'm Ralph Slocum," he said. "This is my wife, Angie. We're plenty obliged to you."

Angie! This Angie Slocum was far different from the Angie Simmons, the young, high-spirited girl who had died that day in Ohio from the bullet of a madman. But the name brought back the hurt, the desolation. This Angie was the mother of four children. She was growing careworn. Her cotton dress, pin-neat, had seen many washings, as had the garb of her husband and children. Luck had never been with the Slocums in the way of accumulating material possessions. This acceptance was in her eyes. But there was also an inner happiness in her and a great pride. She was sustained by the family around her.

She smiled and shook hands with Jeff. "We're mighty indebted to you, Mr. Temple. Chub says you're the best doctor in the world."

"I happened to be able to help," Jeff said. "I'm not a doctor."

The baby in Angie Slocum's arms wriggled and gurgled. The younger boy and his sister stood close to their mother. They were joyfully embarrassed when Jeff spoke to them and poked the lad in the ribs.

Jeff chatted with the parents for a moment or two. "Everybody seems to be having a good time," he said.

Slocum shrugged. "Tonight, at least," he said.

Jeff began to voice the customary amenities as he turned to leave. Slocum halted him. "I take it you're acquainted in these parts, Mr. Temple," he said. "Just what kind of country is it down south of here? These Walkin' Hills?"

"Haven't you been down there?" Jeff asked.

"Only a couple miles. Ain't many of us been farther south than you can walk. Ain't many of us own any horses, an' we don't have money to hire saddlestock."

He added, "From what I've seen, it looks mighty different from what I expected. They say there's really no hills down there."

Jeff considered his answer. "You never reach the Walking Hills," he said. "They just keep walking away from you."

"They tell us we can do well dry farmin' down there," Slocum said anxiously.

"Who told you?" Jeff asked.

Worry clouded Slocum's eyes. And the eyes of his wife. "I reckon a man can grub out a livin' there," he said argumentatively. "Leastwise the railroad wouldn't have fetched us this far an' the government wouldn't be fixin' to open it to entry."

He added, "I never owned any land of my own. It would be real nice."

When Jeff didn't speak, Slocum plunged ahead. "The ranchers ain't goin' to spook us out of it. They don't want to be bothered by farmers, but we don't aim to skedaddle just because they say boo at us."

Jeff thought of the silent men he had seen a few minutes earlier, watching the Zulu camp.

"They've said boo?" he asked.

"Not exactly," Slocum said. "Not in so many words. It's just the way they strut. An' the way they look at us. The way they pack them damned six-shooters. Folks in town tell us nobody packed guns around here any more until us settlers came in. Now everybody goes armed."

He added, his voice rising, "Do they reckon they're the only ones who know how to pull a trigger?"

"Ralph!" his wife protested. "You're talkin' wild."

Slocum subsided. "I guess I get a little too riled at times," he told Jeff. "I fly up, then I cool down. But it gravels me to hear Angie an' my kids called Zulus. It gravels me to have a cattleman look at me like I wasn't fit to walk on the same street with him."

Other men had moved near and were listening. Jeff saw

in them the same anger, the same resentment and determination that was driving Ralph Slocum. These were people who were in too deep to turn back. There had been that same emotion in Peter Mackay. And in Lila Mackay.

He left the Slocums and walked back across the railroad sidings toward the lights of the town. He was still confronted by the purpose that had brought him back to Wardrum. Ramon Montez. Guilty or not, Ramon stood a good chance of going to prison for years. Railroads had powerful influence in the courts and it was standard practice to make examples of men convicted of looting cars.

Jeff debated it. There was one person to whom he could go. It meant asking a favor. A big favor. The man who was in a position to grant that favor would expect this sort of bread, cast on the waters, to be returned sooner or later.

Jeff's thoughts went back to the day he had left Wardrum for college. He had been only nineteen then. His mother, radiant with pride, had kissed him good-by. She had taught school in Wardrum and she had seen to it that he was fully ready for college. She had influenced him to study to become a doctor. She and Alex Crabtree. But he believed that his father had been even happier.

"We'll finally have a Temple who'll know more'n how to follow a flag and carry a gun," Matt Temple had said.

The Temples had followed many flags. A portrait of Jeff's grandfather, who had died at Shiloh, had hung in the parlor of the family home in Wardrum. Alongside it had been a crayon picture of Jeff's great-grandfather, who was buried in some jungle in Central America. He had led a lost cause of liberty in some forgotten revolution. The family Bible had carried the name of an ancestor who had fought in the War of 1812 and of another who had died at Stone Mountain in the Revolutionary War.

That home and all it had contained was gone—burned by some enemy after Matt Temple's death. Except for Jeff and the graves on the knoll there was nothing left here of the Temples or of Matt Temple who had kept law and order in Wardrum for years.

Jeff walked into Hammond Street. New town. Because it was Saturday night, paynight for railroad men, the saloons were busy. Jeff pushed through the swing doors of one named the Open Switch and ordered beer at the bar.

It came in a big glass mug and had been chilled on ice. It was soothing. The darkening mood that had been growing on him eased a trifle.

The patronage consisted mainly of railroad men, with a sprinkling of town people and a few from the settlers' camp who were obviously there to take advantage of any free drinks that might come their way.

There were no cattlemen. Not a spur jingled on the foot-rail at the bar, no cowboy sat at the card tables. Jeff had seen none in Hammond Street. The ranching contingent from the Walking Hills was confining itself strictly to old town on DeSmet Street. New town was for the railroad men—and the Zulus. With the town people nervously trying to cater to both sides.

There were only two men in the place whom Jeff had encountered in the past. He would have passed up this pair without renewing that acquaintanceship except that he became sure they were much more interested in him than seemed necessary. Interested and doing their best to act as though they were unaware of his presence.

Carrying his half-finished mug, Jeff walked to the table where the two sat. "Hello, Professor," he said. "Howdy, Clem. You can now pretend to be surprised at seeing me."

The Professor's name was Ephraim Kelso. He was said to have been a member of the faculty of one of the top eastern universities in the past. A short, corpulent man with a round, jovial face, he had a black plug hat cocked jauntily on his bushy, graying hair. He wore a braid-trimmed frock coat, a gates-ajar collar with a bow tie and an immaculately starched white shirt.

He might have been a plump, mild-mannered clerk. He seemed always slightly flustered and a trifle nearsighted. He was, in fact, a professional, high-play gambler.

He was also exceedingly fast and accurate with a six-shooter when occasion demanded. And occasion had demanded just that at times in the past. Jeff had been a witness to one of these moments.

The Professor's companion was a rawboned individual with stringy, hay-colored hair. He wore a blue gingham shirt and trousers of a gray and white striped pattern that were supported by suspenders and whose cuffs were stuffed into dog-eared cowhide boots. He had a narrow-brimmed felt hat tilted back on his head. His features were angular, with box-like jawbones. He had the appearance of a grass-green tenderfoot. He was anything but that.

"Howdy, Temple," Clem Devore said calmly.

The Professor blinked, then threw back his head with a

roar of laughter. "By the beard of Jupiter!" he boomed. "Jefferson Temple, as I live. Why, my boy, it's been a long time! When was it that we last—?"

"A place called Landslide in the Coeur d'Alene Mountains," Jeff said. "You had a little trouble. Fatal to the other fellow. I testified at the inquest that he'd made the mistake of reaching first."

The Professor beamed. "Of course, of course. I recall the incident very clearly. All of the other witnesses were too timid to speak up. Friends of the gentleman were present at the inquest. They were of a mind to have my neck stretched. You saved me that inconvenience. We had a drink together afterward."

"For which I paid," Jeff said.

"Maybe you didn't do the Professor any favor," Clem Devore said. "Come to think of it, he'd look better if his neck was strung out an inch or two. The way it is, he'd pass for a bullfrog with the mumps."

The Professor smiled benevolently. "Bullfrog with the mumps," he repeated. "Crude, but descriptive perhaps. You coin a phrase at times, Clement."

With a flourish, he motioned Jeff toward a chair. "This calls for a libation," he said.

"Another time," Jeff said. He spoke warily, for there were moments when it was dangerous to refuse to drink with either of this pair. "I've got to talk to a man. I may be back later. If so, I'll take that offer, Professor."

He decided that the Professor was broke—a normal state of affairs with him. "Meanwhile, if you'll accept, I'll have the bartender fetch a bottle. You can return the compliment some other time."

The Professor gazed at him disdainfully. "It happens that I'm in a position to buy my own bottles, Jefferson," he said. "And you along with them. I could buy you, wrap you up like a Christmas turkey, and sell you, if the mood struck me. Observe this."

He drew from a pocket a wad of crumpled greenbacks. He sorted out one and spread it on the scarred poker table, disregarding the wet glass rings. The bill was a fifty-dollar note that had been crisp and new recently, but now was soaking up some of the stale beer and spilled whisky.

Jeff saw that the Professor possessed at least two more of these items. He nodded. "My mistake, Professor. You always were one to save up for a rainy day and old age. Good night, gentlemen."

## CHAPTER FOUR

Jeff walked out of the Open Switch into the cool darkness. If there were two persons in the world whose chances of living to an old age were poor indeed, these were the pair to whom he had just been talking.

He wondered what had brought them to Wardrum. Both had been born under dark stars. Their lives were patched with episodes of violence and gunplay.

The Professor played the part of a genial buffoon, spouting his polished phrases and sometimes delivering informal lectures on literature and the arts.

Clem Devore lived back of the false outer façade of a gawky, uneducated yokel. The truth was that he lived with bitter memories. Jeff had been present on occasions when the Clement Davis Devore of the past had emerged momentarily—a quiet-voiced Virginian, keen-witted and likeable.

It had been nearly a year since he had crossed the trail of either of them. Clem Devore had been working as a lookout for a gambling house in a wild mining camp in Montana at the time. The symbol of his office had been his brace of bone-handled six-shooters. That particular establishment had remained remarkably free of the shootings and crooked gambling that was commonplace in the camp.

Jeff had always felt somewhat indebted to Clem Devore because of this. The camp had been reached by a new branch of the Great Northern and it had been Jeff's business to act as shepherd over the railroad workers who were the sheep for the shearing in the hangouts.

The Professor, at Jeff's last encounter with him about a year previously, had been running a faro bank in Lewiston. Gambling was his customary profession, but when low in funds he had been known to accept pay to work as bouncer in barrooms, a position that he was uniquely qualified to fill.

He was respected by the toughs as much for his strength

as for the dexterity with which he could use a pistol. His appearance of softness was very deceiving. Jeff had seen him lift a husky miner bodily and send him spinning the length of a barroom floor.

Neither Clem nor the Professor had come into open conflict with Jeff, although they had not seen eye to eye on occasions. During one of these moments of friction Jeff had suggested that it would be better for all concerned if they would make themselves scarce at once from a railroad town where they had offended a powerful faction in the rough element and a general riot was in the making.

Jeff had expected them to refuse. They had never been known to back off from trouble, regardless of odds. But they had not made an issue of it. With them, making an issue often meant gunplay. Jeff had told himself many times that he was probably alive because they had not elected to resent being deadlined by him. They had meekly shaken the dust of that particular camp from their feet.

Jeff had no illusions that they were afraid of him. Many men were, but not Clem and the Professor. He had learned the art of making lesser men fear him. It was a necessary part of his business. And also a part of that business was his staying alive.

There had been one or two other occasions when he had intervened for them in certain quarters when they were ticketed for trouble. They had stepped on many toes, earned many enemies. He had seen to it that they had been warned in time to defend themselves in any manner they thought best.

He doubted if they knew he had extended help to them in these cases. However, they seemed to respect him. Perhaps it was his ability with a six-shooter they looked up to—a respect that was mutual. There could hardly be any personal sentiment involved, for it was the harsh creed of men in their calling that no friendships be formed to embarrass them if the cards ran that way. In their view a friend one day might be on the opposite side at the next encounter.

Jeff looked at his watch. The hour was nine-thirty. Late for normal activity, but he knew Bill Hammond's habits. Hammond had always been a night owl, and to him, one day was as good as another when it came to conducting business.

Jeff stopped in an eating house and put away a quick meal, then walked to the railroad depot which was still lighted, awaiting the night train from the junction whose arrival, he had been told, was usually belated.

"Bill Hammond?" the ticket agent echoed in answer to his question. "Why, he don't have offices here at the station. He's got a private palace car deadheaded down in the yards."

"Is that where I'll find him?"

"You ain't been around here long, have you, mister?" the man said. "Bill Hammond don't use that car much. He puts up at the Stockman's Hotel in old town. He set up the Camo general offices there. Took over half a dozen rooms at the upper front upstairs. He'll be up there right now, even on Saturday night. He works seven days a week an' does most of it at night. He's a sundodger."

The man added, grumbling, "Why'n blazes he don't live with railroad people, I'd like to know. The way he toadies to them cattlemen up in old town is a stinkin' shame."

Jeff eyed him. "Bill Hammond toadies to other men? Now you're drawing the long bow, friend."

"An' maybe I'm talkin' too much to a stranger," the man said and hastily turned away.

Jeff walked back up DeSmet Street. The stores were closing for the night. Lila Mackay came hurrying from Louie Cohen's apparel emporium, carrying an armload of bundles. She had a small bonnet perched on her head. It was a very gay affair of yellow straw with a liberal adornment of ribbons and artificial daisies.

She was having trouble balancing the bundles. He grasped her arm, steadying her. "If I didn't know you were a lady I'd say you'd been hitting the jug," he said.

"It's the hat," she said. "It makes me feel giddy."

"I can believe that. You almost ran me down. Which way are you heading? Port or starboard?"

"Straight ahead, sir. Across the tracks."

Jeff arched an eyebrow. She said defensively, "Some of those people need things. A lot of the children don't seem to have too much to wear."

"I better help tote some of these things before you scramble them in the dust," he said. He took over the biggest part of the load and walked with her.

"Who's standing the bill for this?" he asked.

"It doesn't amount to much. Louie Cohen let me have the things at a loss to him. Odds and ends. The remnants of bolts of gingham and calico. Shoes that have been on the shelves for a long time. Stockings, underwear and so on."

Jeff critically eyed the gaudy bonnet. "He threw that in free, of course."

"Don't you like it?" she demanded tragically.

"I'd say it looks something like a rainbow trying to find a home. And without much luck."

"You mean it doesn't look good on me?"

Jeff peered at her. "You're overdoing it. You're the kind that likes to hooraw all the fellows, aren't you?"

She laughed. "I couldn't resist buying it. I saw a girl from the settlers' camp looking at it in Louie's store this afternoon. She was about fourteen. A pretty, wistful little thing. On her, it will look real cute."

"I see."

"I know she wanted it more than anything in her whole life. She's probably never had the kind of a bonnet she's really dreamed about. I remember when I was that age how I longed for one about like this. That one was even brighter."

They crossed the railroad tracks to the Zulu camp. A round dance was in full swing. Lila's step slowed. She suddenly became unsure of herself.

She sighted the Slocums and seized on that as an opening wedge. She hurried ahead. "Chub!" she called.

The Slocums turned, gazing. That was all. They merely stared at her. Other bystanders also turned. There was no friendliness in any of them.

"You are Chub's mother and father, aren't you?" she asked. "My horse injured your dog today. I'm so sorry about it. I wanted to try to make up for it with the children as best I could. I brought them a few presents. Things to wear—and—and—there might be some your neighbors could use . . ."

Her voice had faltered. Jeff saw that she was realizing she had made a sad mistake. Anger had stiffened the faces around her.

"We've got everything we need," Ralph Slocum said grimly. "All of us."

He and his wife turned their backs and rigidly began watching the dancing. Chub hesitated, then followed their example. The younger children stared, frightened.

A shrill-voiced woman among the bystanders spoke. "You're a Mackay, ain't you? We don't want your charity.

Don't try to softsoap us. We know what your kind really think of us."

Jeff noticed a slim, young girl of about fourteen in a calico dress. She was staring at the daisy-bed bonnet with big, longing dark eyes. He saw the struggle between desire and pride. Pride won. She turned away also.

Lila stood looking at their backs. She started to utter a protest, but Jeff touched her arm, drawing her away.

She made one last effort. She lifted the bonnet from her head and walked to where the girl with the wistful eyes stood. "I'd like you to have this, young lady," she said. "It just seems to have been made for you."

The girl could not help looking at the bonnet. The temptation was almost too much for her, Jeff saw. But she resisted it. She tilted her nose and turned away with a flirt of her skirt.

Lila gave up then. Silently she joined Jeff and they walked back across the tracks, carrying the rejected gifts.

"We'll take them back to Louie's," she said. Her eyes were glistening with tears of chagrin. She added, "They're so infernally proud."

"And bitter," Jeff said.

"I'm afraid the bitterness isn't all on their side," she said. "All this means ruin for us. And for them too, but they don't seem to understand that."

"How far has this trouble gone?" Jeff asked.

"There's been nobody killed, if that's what you're asking."

"You mean up to now."

She nodded. "Up to now. So far there's been nothing but some cussing and a few fistfights."

Jeff accompanied her to Louie Cohen's store, where she returned the bundles. "I'll pay for the bonnet, Louie," she said. "If that girl from the Zulu camp comes peeking in the window again, offer it to her if she'll help dust the shelves or something. Make her feel that she's earning it. She won't be able to resist."

Leaving the store they headed toward the Stockman's Hotel, the biggest structure in either new or old town.

"It's been quite a spell since I've sided a real comely girl," Jeff said.

"A pretty speech," she said. "Just how long has it really been?"

Jeff thought of Angie Simmons. "Too long," he said.

She saw the sobering thought in him and didn't pursue

the subject. Her step slowed. She seemed reluctant to end this meeting.

"What can you do to help Ramon Montez?" she asked.

"That's where I'm bound right now," Jeff said. "I want to talk to Bill Hammond. I was told he's set up Camo headquarters in the hotel."

"I hope you're successful," she said.

Her manner and her voice did not seem different. Yet they had changed. Enormously. She was suddenly very distant from him. So distant that it was not bridged by the hand she had laid on his arm while they strolled. She withdrew the hand and they were utterly separated.

"You're probably going to the right place," she said. "Mr. Hammond is quite an important man in these parts."

"But on the side of the Zulus," Jeff said. "And against your people. And against you."

"He's general manager of the railroad," she said. "It's his business to make a success of Camo."

"Why is he at the Stockman's?" Jeff asked. "That's boot and saddle territory. All of old town seems to be."

"Probably as a gesture. He says he's really a cattleman at heart. He seems to be doing his best to smooth down the hackles on both sides."

They paused before the hotel. Its front parlor had wide windows which overlooked the sidewalk. It had plush carpeting and a scatter of leather chairs and sofas, smoking stands and brass cuspidors.

Peter Mackay sat in a chair, a cigar in his mouth, and with him were Evans Johnson and Dan Mulhall, who were Walking Hills ranchers Jeff had known from boyhood. Half a dozen other men were in the parlor. All were cowmen or riders. Some were playing checkers or cards.

"I've got a long spoon," Jeff said.

He saw that she was taken off balance. "They say you need one when you sup with the devil," he explained.

"I've heard that you're able to take care of yourself," she said. "You and Mr. Hammond should hit it off well. You both work for the railroad."

"I'm with Great Northern," Jeff said. "I'm on leave of absence. Great Northern has no connection with Camo."

"Railroad men usually stand together."

"Flock together?"

"If you want to put it that way."

"We may be birds of a feather," Jeff said, "but sometimes we slash and claw at each other."

"Good night," she said. "For Ramon's sake, at least, I hope you have this long spoon you mentioned."

She hurried into the hotel. Jeff watched her blow a kiss to her father as she ascended the inner stairs and vanished above.

An emptiness deadened him. He realized that she had meant this parting to be permanent. He took a stride to follow her and protest. For in her presence he had been completely relaxed and at ease for the first time in longer than he wanted to remember.

It had been like that with Angie Simmons. And with Ramon Montez. There was a phrase for it in cattle country. A person to ride the river with. It went back to the trail days when the big herds were forced to swim the streams that lay across the trail up from Texas. The Red, the Brazos, the Arkansas, the Platte.

A person to ride the river with. A person you could depend on if trouble came. And that was the list. Angie and Ramon.

There was Alex Crabtree, of course. But Alex's backing would always be tempered by judgment. Alex would stay with him whether he was right or wrong and see that he got a square deal, but if he were in the wrong, Alex would see to it that he also paid a just penalty.

His father? Matt Temple, like Alex, had held to unyielding rules of what was right and what was not. Like Alex, his would never have been the unquestioning loyalty of Angie or Ramon.

So short was the list. Lila Mackay's frank eyes kept looking out at him in memory. Strangely, incongruously, the round, florid features of a plump little man wearing a frock coat and a plug hat, and the face of a lantern-jawed, lanky man, came into his thoughts.

He was shocked. It seemed sacrilegious to link men like the Professor and Clem Devore in the same thought with Angie and Lila Mackay.

Yet he had to admit the truth. There was a kinship between himself and these two, the kinship of the six-shooter. But, above all, the Professor and Clem Devore were men who would keep their word. To the death if necessary. And as either an ally or an opponent.

In Lila Mackay he sensed that he had found another

such person. But she was not an ally. She would stay with the opposition. And to the finish.

He halted, knowing that it would be futile to follow her. He moved again to enter the hotel, but this time it was only to go ahead with his intention of seeing Bill Hammond.

Activity up the street caused him to turn. Men were trying to flag down a wild-running horse that carried a weird burden. The animal evaded capture and came galloping nearer.

Jeff ran into the street. Light from store windows reached the horse as it came nearer, and he felt a surge of horror. A tarred and feathered man was clinging to the animal's back.

Jeff leaped and caught the headstall and hung on. He was dragged a dozen yards before the horse gave up. It halted, head down, quivering.

Its rider uttered blubbering, choked words. "God! Git me loose! My God! I'll kill every one of 'em fer this!"

He had been stripped naked and coated with pitch and feathers. His ankles were lashed together beneath the horse which bore no saddle. He had been hanging to the mane so desperately that Jeff had to pry his paralyzed fingers free.

Other men helped cut the lashings and stand the man on his feet. He clung wretchedly to a hitchrail, sobbing and gasping for breath.

Jeff took a neckerchief from a cowhand and cleared the victim's eyes and nostrils. More men were arriving. Peter Mackay came from the hotel and pushed his way to the front of the group.

"Anybody know this fellow?" Mackay asked.

"He looks like one of them Zulus," an onlooker said.

"Hustle to the store and fetch coal oil," Jeff commanded. "Gallons of it. If the store's closed, roust somebody out and have it opened. Fast. Al Winston's barbershop is still lighted. We'll use his bathtub."

"If he's a Zulu, let him go back across the tracks," a man said harshly. "That's where the cuss belongs. His own kind kin take care of him."

The speaker was Tassman Verity, who had been one of the first to run cattle in the Walking Hills. He and Jeff had been well acquainted in the past, but Verity only glared belligerently at him now.

Two men had started to carry out Jeff's order but had

halted. Jeff looked at them and said, "Get going. This poor devil's in misery."

"Let him sweat," Tass Verity said.

Peter Mackay jerked a thumb. "Get goin' boys, an' make it quick." His words seemed to carry the final authority. The two men hurried away.

Tass Verity went stamping away in disgust. "Yo're too soft, Pete," he snarled over his shoulder. "I say to let 'em rot. The whole tribe of 'em."

Jeff led the victim into the back room of the barbershop. The coal oil arrived. He borrowed a slicker and donned it to protect his clothes and set to work.

"One of you boys hustle down to Alex Crabtree's house," he said. "If Alex isn't there, find Aunt Hettie. She'll know what I need. All the cold cream and balsam and sweet oil she can find."

He worked fast. It was a greasy chore, but the patient was soon able to take over the task. The man began to swear in trembling fury. "I'll kill 'em!" he kept repeating. The promise was almost prayerful in its fervency.

"Who are you?" Peter Mackay asked.

The man glared around at the faces of those who crowded the small room. "You all know damned well who I am," he said. "You damned cattlemen call people like me Zulus. It was you who done this to me."

Peter Mackay frowned. "Did you see them?"

"Sure I seen 'em. But they had gunnysacks over their heads. They didn't have the guts to show their faces. But I'll find out who they was, you can bet your bottom dollar on that."

"What's your name?" Mackay asked.

"Carstairs, damn you. Tom Carstairs."

More men crowded into the room. These new arrivals were settlers, Jeff realized. Word of Tom Carstairs' humiliation had reached the Zulu camp. They had invaded old town to see for themselves. Some of them carried pistols and shotguns. Others had clubs and knives.

Jeff got to his feet. "Clear the room!" he commanded. Nobody heeded. Jeff said again, "Clear the room!"

He caught the nearest man by the shirt and gave him a shove. His victim happened to be a rider from one of the ranches.

Providentially Aunt Hettie Crabtree arrived at that moment, personally bringing the supplies Jeff had sent for. She elbowed her way through the grim, angry men. "Git out of here!" she said in her dominating nasal voice. "The lot of you. Didn't you hear what Jeff said? My land, this place is hot as a furnace an' smells like a wolf den. Git, now!"

She was too much for them. The tension eased. Men nearest the door began crowding out of the place. The others followed, flowing into the street.

Peter Mackay lingered a moment. Jeff said, "You're more needed out there than here. If I were you I'd tell your side to talk soft. The Zulus are a mite worked up, and they've got reason to be."

Peter Mackay bristled, for he was not one to take orders. This time he swallowed his pride. He turned and followed the others.

Hettie advanced on the patient. Tom Carstairs, horrified, seized a towel and covered his nakedness. "Get out of here, lady!" he implored. "I ain't got no clothes on."

"Poof!" Hettie brushed Jeff aside. She appropriated the slicker. "I'll take over," she announced. "You've just about got all the tar off his hide, I see. Fetch me some more warm water from out front. I brought castile soap. He can finish up washing himself. I'll spread cream on his hide to take care of the burn. He'll be as good as new in a day or two."

"Lady—!" Carstairs began again helplessly.

". . . and a mighty sight cleaner," Hettie sniffed. "This, likely, is this old sinner's first bath in years. These Zulus!"

Carstairs was reduced to a state of numb acceptance. Jeff washed up and left them, with Hettie spattering soapsuds and Carstairs moaning feebly.

# CHAPTER FIVE

Jeff walked into the street. A sullen knot of settlers remained in sight. The cattlemen had vanished, withdrawing into the hotel. All except Tass Verity. He stood on the sidewalk in front of the Stockman's, a gun on his hip, bushy-tailed and belligerent, inviting any trouble the Zulus might want to start.

Jeff spoke to him. "Tass, better get that bow out of your neck. Peter Mackay's right. This is no time to start trouble." Verity only snorted and walked away from him.

One of the settlers spoke to Jeff. "How's Tom Carstairs?" He was Chub's father, Ralph Slocum.

"He'll be all right," Jeff said.

"Tom will be right obliged to you for helping him," Slocum said. "Fact is, I sort of figured you as a cattleman."

"Why?" Jeff asked.

Slocum shrugged. "Maybe from the looks. You're a doctor, ain't you?"

"I'm neither a doctor nor a cattleman," Jeff said. "What happened? How did Carstairs get into that fix?"

"He pulled out this mornin' to go huntin'. That's about all we know. We ain't had a chance to talk to him."

"Hunting? Where?"

"He said he was goin' to head south apiece. Figured he might pick up a deer. Or even an elk down in these Walking Hills. There's a river down thet way about fifteen miles. The Little Beaver. Tom allowed he'd go that far an' maybe stay a couple o' days."

"That's all cattle country down along the Beaver," Jeff said. "And so is all of the Walking Hills."

Slocum bristled. "It's grazing reserve, but that don't mean it belongs to them. It's still public land. They've got no right to tell us we'll be hung or tarred if we're caught down there."

"Who told you that?"

"It's been whispered around what would happen to us," Slocum snapped. "An' now it's happened."

Another settler spoke. "We ain't takin' no more from them."

"Go easy," Jeff said. "Carstairs likely fell into the hands of some fools who were drunk, or some young cowhands who wanted to be tough. Keep your feet on the ground. It's easy to touch off a big fight. Easy to dig graves. But the regretting isn't easy."

He left them and walked back to the Stockman's Hotel. The parlor was deserted. Only a night lamp burned over the clerk's desk. The cattlemen had swallowed their pride and were doing everything they could to avoid a fight. Guilty conscience, Jeff reflected.

The humiliation of Tom Carstairs could not be justified. It was an act of cowardice that was hardly in keeping with what Jeff knew of the characters of men like Evans Johnson and Dan Mulhall and a few others in the Walking Hills Cattle Association.

He was not so sure about Tass Verity and he knew nothing about Peter Mackay. But, apparently, every man in the Walking Hills would back up the lead of these two.

He ascended to the second floor of the hotel. New, thick, red carpet led to the rooms that had been taken over at the front of the building as the executive offices of Canada & Mexico Overland. Doors with glazed glass panels had been installed, on which were lettered the names of officials. A telegraph sounder clattered in one of these.

All of the other offices were dark and closed except two at the front. One of these bore Bill Hammond's name, along with the announcement that the interior was strictly private. The other door was labeled as the entrance.

Jeff tried the knob of this door. It opened and admitted him into a carpeted, well-appointed anteroom. A young woman of impeccable blonde hair and enameled complexion sat back of a secretary's desk, glaring icily at him.

An open door led into Hammond's private office. Jeff could see cigar smoke drifting there.

"Good evening, ma'am," he said. "Or maybe it is miss? Is Hammond around?"

"*Mr.* Hammond is busy," she said frostily. "If you wish an appointment you will have to come back Monday and state your business."

"Now it's a shame I can't wait that long," Jeff said.

He walked past her into the inner office. Bill Hammond sat tilted back in a big leather swivel chair at a polished flat-top desk. One foot, in an expensive bench-made saddle-boot of alligator leather, was on the desk, the other reclined on a leather hassock. From this restful position Hammond had a view through the window at his side of DeSmet Street and evidently had been watching what had taken place there.

He grinned at Jeff and flicked ashes from the cigar he was smoking. "It's all right, Polly," he called. "Jeff's an old friend."

Two cleaning women in dustcaps and aprons were busy in the room, using brooms and dustcloths.

"That'll do for now, you two," Hammond said. "You can finish up in here later."

The women hastily gathered up their equipment and hurried out.

Jeff eyed Hammond's boots. "Eighty dollars," he estimated.

Hammond laughed. "A hundred. And I got a good price on them at that. They fit like kid gloves."

He swung his feet to the floor and straightened in the chair. "You win the smoke, Jeff."

Jeff selected a cigar from the box of Havanas that Hammond pushed toward him. "Win?"

"For not letting Polly sidetrack you. She overawes the most of them. I put up a cigar with myself that you'd do just what you did. Walk right past her."

"She said you were busy," Jeff said. "Is this a sample?"

Hammond chuckled. "I do the biggest part of my work with my pants planted in a chair. Remember how we used to take care of problems, Jeff? A punch in the jaw, or a rap on the skull with a .45 muzzle. That was the easy way compared to this."

"So you've still got problems."

"Ha! Running a railroad breeds them like maggots."

Jeff used the gold cigar clipper and the lighted taper that floated in a silver bowl. He drew on the cigar.

Bill Hammond liked to consider himself a native of Walking Hills, although he had not been born here and had in fact worked as a riding hand for some of the ranchers for only a few years when he had been in his early twenties.

He was now probably forty-one or forty-two, but looked younger. A big, aggressive-jawed man with crisp, well-barbered brown hair, he was living well. This was beginning to show in the small folds of flesh beneath the chin and above the belt.

He was coatless. His tailored shirt was open at the throat, his tie loosened, for he was the muscular type that burst buttons. He stood six feet one and had weighed two hundred and ten pounds in the days when he had been a pit boss in a Montana copper mine. He was heavier now.

He had held a reputation as a rawhider—a driver of men—but he also took pride in never having asked anyone to take on a chore that he couldn't handle himself, and usually better. He had kept crews on their toes when he had been construction boss on the Great Northern. Jeff had kept them in line in the rowdy towns. That was how they had become well acquainted. Hammond, as did Jeff, bore the scars of those days. The knuckles of his big hands were marked by contact with teeth and skulls. Self-made, self-sufficient, he had a contempt of weakness and a supreme confidence in his own destiny.

He and Jeff had backed each other up on occasions when

real trouble had boiled. Between them, they had always managed to come out of it comparatively unscathed. At least alive. They had played poker together and had celebrated together when such festivity was in order. Yet they had never been close friends. They had never openly clashed, although on many matters their views had been far apart.

"You've moved up, Bill," Jeff said, savoring the aroma of the cigar. "I mind a time when you smoked kinnikinick."

Hammond laughed. "That was when we were snowed in at that camp in the Sawtooths and good tobacco was two hundred miles away."

"How's Camo doing?"

"Standing still right now. We're all set to slam track through the Walking Hills the minute the President signs the bill."

"And then what?"

Hammond eyed him. "How do you mean?"

"What happens after you build through Walking Hills?"

"We'll keep building south. We'll need more financing, naturally. You must be familiar with our plan?"

Jeff was familiar with it. Canada & Mexico Overland's intention, as widely advertised and as its name indicated, was to build from border to border. A vital north and south girder to strengthen the nation was the way Camo put it.

Beginning with the junction with Great Northern, the plan was to link all of the great transcontinental lines. The start had been made at the junction with Great Northern. Next would come the junction with Northern Pacific. Then Union Pacific and the D.&R.G. Then with Santa Fe and finally with Southern Pacific and onward to deepwater ports in Mexico.

It was a grandiose plan. Jeff surmised that Bill Hammond was the author of the glowing pamphlets that Camo broadcast through the East. A stock company had been formed and construction work had started a year previously. Bill Hammond had been in charge, and had pushed steel through to Wardrum in fast time.

Wardrum had come to life. New businesses had sprung up. Gamblers, land speculators and fancy women had arrived. Camo had brought in the Zulus. These were people who had been recruited mainly in the states along the Ohio River, a land where grass grew green and the rivers were fed by abundant rains. They knew nothing about the high, dry plains.

The literature that was being scattered in the East made

it appear that the railroad was still building vigorously ahead. The fact was that it had been stalled at Wardrum for months while the political maneuvering went on in Washington for the charter to enter the Walking Hills.

Jeff was sure that Camo was operating on a thin financial edge. The big, soundly-financed lines, like Great Northern, were staying strictly clear of it and its ambitious plans. These pretentious quarters in the Stockman's were for appearance's sake.

Bill Hammond chuckled as he watched Jeff's expression. "I know what you're thinking. Sure, we're lean. We're hungry. There never was a new railroad that wasn't. But that'll change when the Hills are settled. Look at Oklahoma since the big runs. We'll get fat too."

"This isn't Oklahoma," Jeff said. "What will these people do for a living?"

"Farm, of course. Raise wheat."

"And eat snowballs," Jeff said. "You know there's no money in wheat on a hundred and sixty acres. Not in this country. No more than there is in running cattle in the Walking Hills unless you've got lots of range. It takes fifty acres or more to range a cow down there."

Hammond uttered a roar of laughter. "You must have been listening to Pete Mackay. Or Tass Verity."

"I know the Hills," Jeff said.

"I believe you punched cattle for Tass Verity a time or two," Hammond said. "He and Pete Mackay are my biggest headaches. Between them they control two thirds of the country down there. The other outfits are small-bore. They'll do what Tass and Pete tell them to do."

"Tass and Pete? Just like that. Do they call you Bill?"

"Of course," Hammond said impatiently. "Personally, they're fine men. It's only that they're riding a dead horse. I don't blame them for not wanting to give up a good thing. They only own one acre in a hundred of what they use. They bought up all the proved land along Little Beaver, then wrangled the government into withdrawing the rest of it as grazing reserve. But times change. They've got to move out."

"Where'll they go?" Jeff asked.

"Frankly, I don't know," Hammond admitted. "They've got a problem, I must admit."

"They don't seem in the mood to pull out."

"That's the problem of the government," Hammond said.

"It looks like it might be the problem of these Zulus. At least one of them already has had his put to him."

Hammond frowned. "You mean that poor devil who was tarred and feathered? I saw all of that from the window. It's hard to believe Pete Mackay and Tass Verity would have anything to do with a thing like that."

"Whether they did or not, they're going to be blamed," Jeff said. "You just gave the why-for. They're the big augurs in the cattle association."

"You mean that fellow might try to get square?"

"He said he'd kill the men who tarred him. His name is Carstairs. He struck me as a tough old bird who'd do just what he said."

"Apparently you got here just at the right time, Jeff," Hammond said.

Jeff eyed him. "How's that?"

"I've got a job for you. Six hundred a month and unlimited expenses."

"That's a nice sum," Jeff said. "What's the title?"

"Special agent. The same job you held with G.N."

"This job?" Jeff asked. "You want me to see that no more of your sheep are tarred and feathered?"

"They're not exactly sheep," Hammond said. "Your job is to see that they don't go gunning for cattlemen."

"Or vice versa," Jeff said.

"There's no cause for bloodshed. You're to keep the peace. That's all."

"If this thing ever gets rolling, one special railroad agent won't last long," Jeff commented.

"You'll have help," Hammond said.

"I'm not taking the job."

"Ephraim Kelso and Clem Devore are working for Camo," Hammond said. "Good men. They'd be quite a lot of help to you."

"So that's why they're in town," Jeff remarked. "Then that was Camo money the Professor was flashing in a saloon tonight?"

"You'll admit, Jeff," Hammond said, "that they'd be mighty handy to have on your side."

"I'm not in this," Jeff said. "I came here on something else. A friend of mine needs a little help."

"Friend? Would I know him?"

Jeff eyed Hammond for a moment. "Ramon Montez," he said slowly. "I'm sure you've heard of him."

"Montez? Montez? Why, of course. He's the—"

"The man charged with stealing a bunch of .44-40 Winchesters and a couple of thousand rounds of shells from a

Camo express car. On top of that he's charged with trying to kill one of your Camo agents when some of them tried to roust him and his wife around at the time they searched his place and found the stuff."

"So he was a friend of yours?" Hammond drawled.

Jeff leaned back in his chair. "You know, Bill," he said. "I should have known better than to underestimate you."

Hammond nodded. "You really should have, Jeff."

Jeff began telling off the points on his fingers. "Camo got its guns back. And the ammunition. I take it this hardware was brought in for some purpose. To arm the Zulus, most likely. Ramon is in jail. Because Ramon is in jail, I am here in your office and we are asking mutual favors of each other."

Hammond only continued to chuckle, enjoying this.

"The fool who broke his leg when Ramon shot his horse from under him had it coming," Jeff said. "Ramon should have killed him. The fellow tried to get gay with Dolores."

Hammond nodded. "That man will never make the same mistake again. I beat hell out of him, personally, then fired him. We don't pick on women, Jeff."

"Only on men," Jeff said. "Ramon has more than Dolores to worry about if he's sent up. They've got two children."

"Tough," Hammond said. "He should have thought of that before he broke into that car."

"Ramon says the stuff was planted in his haystacks."

"Nobody's ever guilty of anything," Hammond said scoffingly. "It's always either a case of mistaken identity, or they say they were framed."

"Ramon could get ten years," Jeff said.

"Twenty, if the judge is tough," Hammond said. "One section of that express car was carrying mail."

"And the judge will be tough," Jeff said. "Federal judges in this neck of the woods bear down on people who rob railroads. The railroads help pay their salaries."

Hammond leaned forward. "Look, Jeff! You were right. After all, Camo lost nothing. If this Montez is a good friend of yours I'll have our lawyers withdraw the charges. I'll see to it tomorrow. No, that's Sunday. Monday, then."

He grinned. "Strictly as a favor to you, of course. Montez means nothing to me. Not a thing. You scratch my back, Jeff, I scratch yours."

Jeff was remembering the interest the Professor and Clem

Devore had taken in him in the Open Switch. Evidently they had known all along that they might be allies.

"The next time you send a telegram to me, Bill," he said. "Sign your own name, not Doc Crabb's."

Hammond didn't bother to deny the forgery. "This will be an easy job. There'll be no trouble. Not with you and the Professor and Clem Devore around. The sheriff here is a weakling."

"Lish Carter a weakling?" Jeff said ironically. "Come now. Furthermore Lish is a cattleman. He'll be on their side."

"No matter," Hammond said. "All Camo asks is a fair deal. Take it or leave it."

"If I leave it then Ramon does twenty years?"

Hammond extended a hand across the table. "Then it's a deal."

Jeff ignored the hand. "How many have the other side hired?" he asked.

"Pete Mackay surely wouldn't go that far!" Hammond protested.

"Then Tass Verity would," Jeff said. "Or are you trying to hooraw me into believing Camo is the only side entitled to hire men to do its fighting?"

"I can't believe they would," Hammond insisted.

"Maybe," Jeff said. "It's a nice thought to hold."

He arose and picked up his hat. "You always were pretty good at thinking, Bill. Well, I'll drift along."

"Your pay started as of a week ago," Hammond said. "You can draw in advance. Polly will give you a voucher."

"This one," Jeff said, "is on me. There'll be no charge, Bill, outside of keeping your word about turning Ramon loose."

He chucked the blonde secretary under the chin as he passed through the anteroom. "Pretty Polly," he said. "I'll fetch you a cracker the next time."

"And lose a thumb," she snapped.

She sat watching him walk on through the door into the hall. It occurred to Jeff that she was waiting—wanting to make sure he was gone before making whatever was her next move.

He halted after taking a few strides down the hall and turned back, his steps silenced by the green runner of carpet underfoot.

He had not bothered to close the door of the anteroom when he had left. He halted alongside the opening. Polly had left her desk and had come hurrying to close the door. She discovered him there. She was obviously dismayed and also angered. She closed the portal hurriedly, but not before he caught a glimpse of a lean, weathered man in the garb of a cattleman who was just entering Hammond's inner office.

Hammond's visitor was Tassman Verity, owner of the big Block T in the Walking Hills, who, along with Peter Mackay, was the bulwark of the opposition to the opening of the range to homesteading.

There could be many reasonable explanations, of course, for Verity's meeting with Hammond. For one thing, Hammond had said that he was friendly with both Tass Verity and Peter Mackay.

Still, there had been furtiveness about Verity's manner. He had not wanted to be seen in the Camo offices. Also, his business had been important. Evidently he had been waiting out of sight somewhere for Jeff to leave. The blonde secretary had been poised to summon him the instant the coast was clear.

## CHAPTER SIX

Jeff descended into DeSmet Street. The dance at the Zulu camp was still on. He could hear the music. He walked down the street, turned into new town and entered the Open Switch on Hammond Street.

The Professor and Clem Devore still sat at the card table. The Professor was playing solitaire. Devore had his chair tilted against the wall, his heels hooked in the rungs. His hat was well down over his eyes. He apparently was dozing, but he was keenly awake.

Both men, Jeff realized, had been awaiting his return. He pushed a chair with its back against the table and straddled it.

"What'll it be?" Clem Devore asked.

"Beer," Jeff said. He waited while Devore signaled a bartender who brought three filled mugs.

Jeff drank from the mug, then placed it on the table. "That's my limit for tonight," he said. "And every night. We will all hold it down to beer. And only one or two a day. That goes for as long as we're in Wardrum. Just enough to keep the dust out of our gullets. Whiskey might warp our judgment."

"Now that's just what I was tellin' the Professor," Clem said complainingly. "I said to him, this fella's goin' to put us on the Injun list when he comes back."

Jeff smiled. The Injun list was the tally of names that bartenders kept of men to whom, for various reasons, it was not advisable to sell liquor.

"Then you two knew I'd be back?" he asked.

The Professor swept the cards together with disgust. "It's enough to drive a man to chicanery," he grumbled. "One card was all I needed and it stubbornly refused to come up."

"Maybe your luck will run the other way against other cards I could mention," Clem Devore said soothingly. "Arch Stanton, for instance."

Jeff spoke. "Arch Stanton? He's in town?"

"He sure is," Clem said. "Along with Bass Brackett and Fletch Jones. I saw 'em on the street this evenin'."

The warning was plain enough. Clem Devore was saying that the cattlemen were importing fighting men. And men of tough fiber at that. Arch Stanton and Bass Brackett had locked horns with Jeff in the past at Lewiston when Jeff was seeing to it that railroad men got a fair shake in a gambling house. The dispute had passed over before it had reached the shooting stage.

If Clem and the Professor knew that Stanton and others were in town and on cattle pay, then Bill Hammond must have known it also. He had not wanted to admit that in bringing Jeff to Wardrum he was aiming on fighting fire with fire.

"Any others?" Jeff asked.

The Professor answered. "None that we've seen." He riffled the cards and spread a new solitaire layout. The cards flipped from his hands in a swift cascade, each alighting exactly in its rightful place. "But there are bound to be more," he said. "Indubitably."

"How deep's your stake in this?" Jeff asked.

"Two hundred dollars per month," the Professor said. "Two months pay guaranteed."

"Same here," Clem said. "I've done better. I've done worse."

"How's your family, Clem?" Jeff asked.

The Professor's pudgy hands paused for a moment in

handling the cards, then resumed. Clem Devore's head lifted. His face was no longer slack-eyed or artless. It was a lean, hard, bitter face. His eyes were ice blue.

"I've known about it for a long time, Clem," Jeff said.

Clem sat stonily silent. But he was a man with his soul in torment. Some four years in the past he had tried to do what many men had attempted in vain. He had sought to be born again—to shed the past along with its mistakes and its grudges and start anew.

He had fallen in love with a decent young woman he had met during a trip to Seattle. She had not known that he was Clem Devore, the notorious gunman of the boom towns. They had married and he had not gone back to his old haunts in the mountains and on the plains. He had found a job on the Seattle docks among men of the sea, where the chances of meeting anyone from the past seemed very remote. He and his bride lived quietly in a rented house that they intended to buy some day.

Clem had become the father of a son when the past overtook him. It was an amazing parallel to the way Jeff's parents had died. A man who held a grudge from the past had sighted Clem on the street and had trailed him to his home. After dark, the man had crept to a window and shot at Clem, who was sitting at the supper table with his wife and baby.

The bullet had missed Clem. It had not missed his wife nor the baby in her arms. It had killed the baby and had passed on through the mother's body. It had damaged the spine of the mother, leaving her a paralyzed invalid.

Clem had killed the man as he tried to escape. He had emptied his gun into the man's body in screaming despair. A coroner's jury had exonerated him, but there was no easy way out for his conscience, for since that night his wife had been doomed to spend her days in a wheelchair.

Jeff knew that she was being given the best of care in a home in Seattle that Clem maintained and where he spent all the time he could. He had brought specialists from the East, hoping that the miracle could be worked. He had put out big sums on nature fakers and charlatans. He had never given up the search, nor the hope.

All this had cost money. Clem had gone back to his trade of selling his services as a fighting man. He was considered always worth his price. Merely his presence and his reputation were usually enough to calm troubled waters.

"How did you know this?" Clem asked harshly.

"A doctor friend of mine," Jeff said. "We had been students together. He's a company doctor for Great Northern. He told me in strictest confidence."

The Professor turned over a card and at the same time his elbow pushed back the flap of his long coat so that the black handle of a holstered six-shooter was unobstructed.

"We have company," he murmured.

Behind him Jeff heard the jingle of spurs and the wooden thump of bootheels as new patrons entered the Open Switch and walked to the bar.

Clem Devore spoke casually, "That black queen will play on the red king, Ephraim."

The Professor scowled in fierce reproof. "The cardinal joy of solitaire is that it be played alone, Clement. Kindly refrain from cadging on my pastime."

Jeff glanced over his shoulder. Four men were lining up at the bar. One was Arch Stanton. With him was the burly, black-mustached Bass Brackett and the small, pasty-faced, smooth-shaven Fletcher Jones. The fourth man was a stranger. He had dusty, sorrel-colored hair and a small red mustache and sideburns.

All wore the garb of ranch hands, but Arch Stanton preferred a little more flash than the dark, hardtwist breeches and blue flannel shirts of the others. He had on a suede vest, patterned with Indian beads, a sand-colored, wide-brimmed hat with a steeple crown, and foxed, tailor-made breeches that narrowed into hand-stitched yellow boots. He was a big, lithe man with a lot of even white teeth in his smile and he never had to look far for feminine companionship.

"The red jack on the black queen, Ephraim," Clem said. In a lower voice to Jeff, "The *alazan* goes by the name of Red Kramer."

Jeff tightened inwardly. He presently wheeled and took another look at the *alazan*. That was the Spanish word for sorrel. This was his first personal meeting with the man who had been exonerated of the murder of his parents. Exonerated by perjury everyone believed.

Their eyes met and held for a moment. Kramer's were the first to shift away. Jeff was sure that the man was aware of his identity and had deliberately invited this meeting. But Kramer had suddenly found himself not so sure he wanted to be here after all.

Jeff looked at Clem and the Professor. Clem murmured, "Cattle association fighting men. What else?"

Arch Stanton poured drinks and said loudly, "Here's to frolic and damnation." He refilled his glass, turned and pretended he had just discovered the presence of Jeff and his companions.

"Jeff Temple!" he exclaimed. "And the Professor and Clem Devore!"

He came walking down the room to their table, the whisky sloshing over the rim of his glass, its rankness strong in the air. He downed the remainder of the drink, gagged, and said, "I haven't seen any of you boys in quite a spell. What brings you to Wardrum?"

"Wind blowing in the right direction," Jeff said. "We just hoisted sail and here we are."

"The last I heard of you, you were a G.N. rawhider," Stanton said.

"Times change," Jeff said. "So does the wind."

"Mind if I sit and palaver about old times?" Stanton asked.

"Pull up a chair," Jeff said. "But don't jumble up the Professor's cards. He's on his way to winning and he's touchy."

Stanton hooked a chair from another table with a foot and brought it skidding into place. He was about to sit down when Bass Brackett called from the bar, "Let's move along, Arch. There's a faro game at the Silver Bell that I always make money at."

Stanton was about to refuse. Then he changed his mind. "All right," he said and arose. To Jeff, he said, "Another time. You'll be around awhile, I hope."

"No telling," Jeff said.

He watched Stanton and his companions leave. They had been joined by a fifth man who was a stranger to Jeff.

"Now who do you reckon sent for 'em?" Clem said thoughtfully.

"That last one who came in?" Jeff questioned.

Clem nodded. "He came into this place in a hurry, said something to Brackett, an' Brackett gave Stanton the wink."

Jeff arose, walked out on the sidewalk. But Stanton and his comrades had already vanished somewhere. There seemed little point in trying to locate them and he returned to the table in the Open Switch.

He sat there, sipping the remainder of the beer, his eyes on the Professor's card game, but his mind wrestling with a long list of complex questions. The only answers he could reach were unpleasant.

"What remuneration did our friend, Hammond, offer you, Jefferson?" the Professor asked, breaking a long silence.

"Six hundred a month," Jeff said.

"Something," the Professor said thoughtfully, "tells me that you refused."

"The money, yes," Jeff said. He sat for a time, then added, "The job, no."

The professor wagged his head. "Strange. You would be worth every cent of it to Camo. And far more. Your father was a friend of Teddy Roosevelt, so I'm told."

Jeff looked at him, then slapped a hand angrily on the table. "Of course. Of course."

"You might be a valuable asset to Camo when Roosevelt comes to making a decision about opening the Walking Hills," the Professor said. "It's the small things that sometimes sway important decisions. The name of a Temple on a Camo payroll would impress even a President, perhaps."

They all went silent, for the report of a gunshot had come echoing against the walls of the town.

More shooting came. A volley, the reports solid and reverberating in the night. Jeff heard the screaming in the distance of terrified women and children. And the yelling of infuriated men.

He exclaimed, "The Zulu camp!"

The three of them arose and went hurrying out of the Open Switch. The shooting was continuing in the camp. And the screaming. Jeff broke into a run. Clem kept step with him, but the Professor was not up to such exertion and followed at a more sedate pace.

They crossed the railroad yards, scrambled over the couplings of the line of sidetracked cars and came into view of the camp. Four or five of the shacks and tents were on fire, with settlers swarming around, trying to save what they could of the contents.

Riders were galloping out of the camp, heading for the brush downstream. They wore gunnysacks over their heads, pierced with eyeholes. Below that were yellow slickers. Their horses had been smeared with red mud to balk identification.

Jeff sighted at least five riders. They were scattering through the outer fringe of the camp, using willows and scrub cottonwood to cover their flight. Evidently their guns were empty for they had quit shooting.

Someone in the camp opened up in belated retaliation, using a rifle. Jeff heard five shots pumped at the fleeing raiders.

One of the masked men was hard hit. He clung to the horn for a moment, then fell limply to the ground. His horse went racing onward in the darkness in the wake of the escaping raiders.

The rifleman in the Zulu camp fired a final shot at the last of the raiders as he was spurring through the brush. Jeff saw the man grasp convulsively at his left arm. He recovered and rode on out of sight into the brush.

Jeff and Clem moved warily into the camp, risking the chance that some excited settler might misinterpret their intentions and take a shot at them. Men were beginning to emerge cautiously from cover. Children were wailing. Some of the women were still screaming hysterically.

"Damned cattlemen!" a man frothed. "Ridin' like wild Injuns! Skeerin' women an' kids half to death."

"Anybody hit?" Jeff asked.

"I don't know," the man said. "Them fellers seemed to be shootin' in the air mostly."

"The livin' hell they was shootin' in the air!" another man screeched. "They killed Jennie Barnes! There she lays, right in her own doorway, shot right through the heart. The hell they was shootin' high! The—the, oh, God! The damned murderers!"

Jeff and Clem watched the settlers lift the calico-clad body of a middle-aged, graying woman and carry it into one of the shacks.

From the babbled accounts, Jeff gathered that the raiders had swept in without warning while the dance was going on. They had dragged firewads made of burning oil-soaked waste taken from the wheels of railroad cars and had hurled them into tents and onto the roofs of shacks.

"Get a bucket brigade going or you'll loose some more shacks," Jeff shouted, and began pushing men into action.

Clem called to him. "Come here!"

The Professor had joined them. He and Jeff walked to where Clem stood beside the body of the masked raider who had been shot from his horse. The man was dead.

Clem pulled off the gunnysack hood on which blood was already stiffening. The bullet had torn through the man's lungs and he hadn't lived many seconds after he had toppled to the ground. He was a lean, hard-featured man with stringy brown hair. His pistol lay beside him. Jeff picked it up and examined it. Every shell in the cylinder had been fired.

Ralph Slocum came walking up, trying to reload a rifle. It was one of the reliable old .44-40 Winchesters, a gun that had been a stand-by on the frontier for many years. Slocum was having a hard time at the task, for his hands were shaking.

"I killed this one," Slocum chattered. "I never shot at a human bein' in my life until now. An' the first bullet I let go at one killed a man."

He drew a deep, quivering breath. "I've got no real load on my conscience," he said. "He had it comin'."

"Nobody will try to hold you to account for it," Jeff said.

"It was the other one I was tryin' to git," Slocum said. "This man rode into the line o' fire. I kept shootin' but I only winged the other one. He was the one that murdered poor Jennie Barnes. He done it deliberately."

"Deliberately?"

"I'd swear on the Bible he did," Slocum said. "Jennie was so skeered she was just standin' there. Like she was paralyzed. Right there in the door of her own place. Starin' at them devils. This one rode past. Then, I saw him swing his horse around an' ride back so as to kill her."

"That's hard to believe," Jeff said. "Are you sure?"

"It happened right before my eyes. He took aim an' shot her down with a pistol. I'd been so damned skeered myself up to that time I hadn't been able to think right. That woke me up. I run into my shack, got my rifle an' tried to bring him down. I only got him in the arm. The left arm. I saw him grab at it as he rode away."

Slocum added, "But I'd know the devil if I ever laid eyes on him ag'in."

"You could identify him?"

"The same way Jennie did," Slocum snapped. "That's why he killed her."

Slocum decided he was talking too much. He forestalled Jeff's next question. "I know what I know," he said. "An' I'll tell it when the proper time comes."

Jeff and Clem straightened the twisted body of the dead man.

"Maybe we kin find out somethin' about him an' who he is," Slocum said.

Clem began searching the man's pockets. These produced the usual personal effects, trinkets, keepsakes and tobacco. Also a worn wallet.

"Any name?" Jeff asked. But Clem shook his head.

"I know him," the Professor said. "He worked as a bouncer in dance halls in Lewiston a few years back. They called him Reelfoot. He hailed from Tennessee."

There was money in the wallet. Clem counted the bills, then replaced them in the billfold and returned them to the man's pockets. "Ashes to ashes," he said. "They all go the same way, sooner or later. All of us."

Sheriff Lish Carter arrived and began asking questions and taking notes. But his activity was superficial. Jeff saw that Carter had no intention of making a real investigation. Ozzie Stone, the Wardrum furniture dealer who also acted as coroner and undertaker, appeared and took charge of the bodies.

Jeff waited while the sheriff talked lengthily with Ralph Slocum. Lish Carter evidently had in mind arresting Slocum and locking him up in jail. He quickly abandoned the idea. The settlers were in no mood to stand for it.

As Bill Hammond had said, they were no longer sheep. The raid had done something for them. It had tempered their steel, fused them together. It had been the final affront, the ultimate gesture of contempt for them that had brought their pride to the fighting point.

"No damned cattleman better ever set foot in this camp ag'in," a brawny settler told the sheriff. "You're elected by cattlemen. You dance to their music. See to it that you don't swing on the same rope with them. You ain't arrestin' Ralph or anybody else. It was self-defense against an unjustified assault, an' there's a hundred witnesses here to testify to it. They'll do so at the proper time an' place."

Lish Carter looked at Jeff and Clem and the Professor. "An' three more'n a hundred, I reckon," he said bitingly. "The worse of the lot."

The sheriff soon pulled out, accompanying the coroner's black wagon in which Reelfoot's body was carried away.

Jeff drew Ralph Slocum aside. "You said you could identify the man who killed Jennie Slocum."

"Sure," Slocum said warily. "He's got a bullet in his arm."

Jeff could see that this was all he would get out of him. "All right," he said. "Play it your way."

"Which side are you three on?" Slocum demanded.

"The sheriff seems to figure we're backing you people," Jeff said.

"And how do you figure it?"

"From the way the wind keeps blowing, it looks like he could be right," Jeff said.

"This wind," said the Professor, "has considerable influence."

"Maybe we don't need any help," Slocum said. "Meanin' no offense, of course. I'm not forgettin' your kindness to my kids, Mr. Temple."

"Let's hope you're right," Jeff said.

The bucket brigade was extinguishing the embers of the structures that had burned. A considerable array of weapons was in sight. Some had pistols, but the majority of the Zulus, like Ralph Slocum, possessed .44-40 rifles. Jeff surmised that these had been furnished by Camo from the shipment Ramon Montez was accused of stealing.

Jeff and his companions headed across the tracks toward new town. The Professor spoke. "It isn't like you, Clement," he said reprovingly, "to filch money from a dead man. What was your motive in extracting that banknote from Reelfoot's purse?"

"Dang your sharp eyes," Clem said calmly. "Maybe I only wanted to make sure of his funeral expenses. Money has a way of disappearin' from dead men's pockets once they fall into the hands of strangers."

"Very humanitarian," the Professor said.

"I hope somebody will do the same for me if it turns out that way," Clem said. "I have a bad dream that keeps comin' back. I see me left lyin' for the buzzards. Sometimes it's the wild hogs that get me."

The Professor shuddered. "You *do* have morbid dreams. I regret mentioning the matter. Now *I'll* have nightmares."

Silhouetted against the lights of the town, Jeff saw a feminine figure in the darkness ahead. He left his companions and walked to confront Lila Mackay, who was picking her way across the tracks toward the Zulu camp.

"Do you make a habit of wandering around places like this at all hours of the night?" he snapped.

"It would seem that way," she said.

"You're supposed to be in bed."

"I couldn't sleep," she said. She was under great strain.

She started to move past him but he blocked the way. "You'd better not go down there," he said.

"What happened there? All that shooting? And there were fires."

"Some drunks thought it would be fun to hooraw the Zulus."

She kept looking at him, demanding an answer to a question she did not want to put into words.

Jeff could not refuse. "Yes," he said reluctantly. "Two people were killed. One was from the bunch that ran the raid."

Again he saw in her an urgent question and an insistence on an answer. "The man was a drifter they called Reelfoot," he said. "A woman was killed too."

"A woman? Oh, no!" She shuddered and was silent for a space. "I keep thinking about the Slocums," she said. "Those cute little children."

"None of them were hurt," Jeff said.

He took her arm. She hesitated, then let him walk her back into the town. He did not head directly for the hotel. He turned down a side street off DeSmet and circled a dark block in the back area of old town. He felt some of the tautness fade out of the arm he kept linked in his own.

"Pat McCarthy's blacksmith shop," he said as they passed a dark structure. "At least that's still the same. The same old smell of soot and singe and hoof burn. It was only yesterday that I used to stand and watch the sparks fly from the anvil and wait for them to turn into gold nuggets. Somebody told me they would. I guess he was only stringing me."

"I'd say you were about nine or ten years old yesterday," she said. "That's the age when you believe in all the good things. That's when it's easy to think that sparks will turn into gold nuggets."

"And not into buzzards and hogs," Jeff said.

She appraised him. "Now that's a strange thing to say."

"This isn't yesterday."

"No," she said wearily. "This is another day. And we're grown up."

They returned to DeSmet Street. Charlie Kelly's billiard parlor was still open. Through the window Jeff saw that only one table was being used. The players were Arch Stanton and Bass Brackett. Sitting in the chairs that lined the walls were Fletcher Jones and Red Kramer, beer bottles in their hands. All were in shirt sleeves, their saddle jackets hanging on wall hooks. They had the attitudes of having been there for some time. At least one thing was sure. None had a bullet-wounded left arm.

After they had walked onward for a distance, Lila asked, "Who are they?"

He looked at her. "Don't you know?"

"No. Should I?"

"Then it doesn't matter," he said.

When they reached the steps of the hotel she paused and stood for a time without speaking. "Good night!" she finally said.

She started to turn away, then halted. "The Zulus *are* wrong, you know!" she burst out.

"Tarring and feathering them won't help right it," Jeff said. "Nor killing their women. Blood's been spilled."

"And there'll be more. That's what you mean, isn't it?"

"Who knows?"

"But you are against us. You're for the Zulus—for Camo. You've been hired."

She ran up the steps into the darkened parlor of the hotel without looking back. Except for the night lamp, all of the hotel was dark and silent. The upper front windows where Bill Hammond's Camo offices were located were now black and unlighted.

Jeff turned away. She had stated it bluntly. He was on Camo's side, and against the cattlemen. Against her father. Scratch my back and I'll scratch yours, Bill Hammond had said. There was no other way to help Ramon Montez.

It was a fantastic situation. The cattlemen had their backs to the wall. In many ways they had right and justice on their side. But their methods were wrong. They were apparently stubbornly convinced they could bulldoze the Zulus into pulling out. They didn't seem to realize that they were only goading their quarry into fighting back.

Furthermore their methods were certain to turn public opinion against them, and particularly the opinion of the White House, which was where it would count the most.

Jeff believed the Zulus were following a mirage that would leave them stranded in a hostile land. But they too, for the most part, were sincere and honest people. Whatever their ignorance of conditions in the Walking Hills, they were of pioneering fiber. They had the inner toughness to venture into new lands.

Although they seemed at opposite poles in viewpoint and temperament, the Zulus and the cattlemen were akin fundamentally. They were all visionaries—empire builders. They were men and women who had the courage to gamble with the unknown, to pit their strength against nature itself.

That was why the situation offered terrible possibilities. All the elements were here of strength of will meeting unyielding pride. Internecine strife, the saddest of all forms of warfare, could be the outcome.

"Over here," the Professor's voice spoke.

He and Clem Devore were waiting in the darkness of a store entrance across the street.

Jeff, annoyed, joined them. "You're being a little nosey," he said.

"She's a mighty fetching young lady," the Professor said.

Clem spoke. "A pretty piece of calico can sure play hell with a man's aim at times. Just by the flutter. Jiggles him right off the target."

"Keep out of my personal affairs," Jeff said.

"Even in midstream men sometimes change horses, Jefferson," the Professor said mildly.

"Not always because of the flutter of calico," Jeff said. "Sometimes a man might decide he's on the wrong horse."

The Professor sighed. "Scruples. You still have them, apparently."

Jeff shrugged. "They're a handicap, I admit. But I'm afraid I have them."

"Good!" Clem said, and laid a hand on Jeff's shoulder.

Jeff was surprised. "Good?"

"Elucidate, Professor," Clem said.

"Clement keeps pilfering my very best words," the Professor complained. "What we mean is that we feel that a man with scruples can be depended on to let us know just where he stands."

"Some men we've worked with," Clem explained, "had money from the other side in their pockets at the time. But we didn't know it until we about got a slug in our backs."

"Apparently I'm not the only one who's burdened with scruples," Jeff said. "You two are handicapped too."

The Professor removed his plug hat and made a sweeping bow. "We assure you that we will let you know where we stand—at any and all times."

It was a compact. A compact that they stand together, or forewarn the others if their loyalty shifted.

"Where are you stayin'?" Clem asked.

"I haven't pitched camp yet," Jeff said. "I left my warbag at the depot. That reminds me, I better claim it before they close up for the night."

"We'd be honored if you would share with us our humble abode," the Professor said.

"Where is it?" Jeff asked.

"Like yourself, we haven't actually moved in yet," the Professor said. "We are temporarily quartered at a modest rooming house. A fleabag, in fact. But we have another choice."

"This other place ain't nothin' much either," Clem said. "Velvet curtains, thick carpets, plate glass, linen you can make snowballs out of and a flunky to wait on you. Solid silver on the table. Even a finger bowl."

The Professor explained. "It happens that a gentleman offered us the use of his private palace car during our visit here. We've debated accepting."

"Bill Hammond's private car," Jeff said. "I was told he wasn't using it himself. He's putting up at the Stockman's."

"Fact is there'll be a bed all fixed up for you," Clem said. "A berth, they call it in a railroad car, I reckon. We were told to let you know that you could make yourself at home."

Bill Hammond had been very sure of me, Jeff reflected. "Such luxury might spoil me," he said. "I'm going to stay with an old friend. A doctor. Alex Crabtree."

He felt better, a trifle more free of soul in even this small refusal to further obligate himself to Bill Hammond.

He peered closer at them, sensing something in them that was unspoken. Then the answer came to him. "The doctor has a big house," he said. "Plenty of beds. Any friends of mine will be more than welcome. You'll feel at home there. Whenever I was in Wardrum after my folks were gone I stayed at the Crabtree house."

"We wouldn't want to impose on the good doctor," the Professor said.

"Not by a long shot," Clem said emphatically.

They wanted to accept. Like himself, Jeff realized they were squirming under Bill Hammond's thumb.

"Get your stuff," he said.

"You certain for sure we'd be welcome?" Clem protested.

It came to Jeff that what was swaying them was this word. Welcome. It was a scarce item in men of their calling. It came to Jeff that he had not heard it mentioned also for a long time.

Like the Professor and Clem he was a loner, a man to be given an ingratiating slap on the back and a pretense at real friendliness, but never to be admitted to the inner circles of the lives of others. Fawned upon openly and feared covertly.

"Meet me here in fifteen minutes," Jeff said. "The Crabtree house is in walking distance."

He quit talking. The three of them silently watched a blocky-shouldered man cross the unlighted street nearly a block away and enter the hotel. Peter Mackay. He was wearing a denim saddle jacket.

Mackay had been somewhere in the town instead of asleep in his room at the time of the raid on the Zulu camp. Jeff knew that it had been her father Lila had been hunting when he had intercepted her.

Jeff and his companions scattered to gather up their luggage. Jeff retrieved his suitcase and saddlebag at the depot and returned to the meeting place.

A rider left the livery stable, where only a night lantern burned, and turned down a side street southward.

Again it was Peter Mackay. His visit at the hotel had been short. At that distance it was impossible to make out much about him, except that he was still wearing the jacket. Its sleeves covered both of his arms to the wrists.

Mackay carried a rifle slung under an arm. His right arm. Then he was gone from sight.

# CHAPTER SEVEN

It was Aunt Hettie, a wrapper over her nightrobe, her hair in curlers, who appeared when Jeff twisted the key on the brass bell of the locked front door.

Years of answering summonses at all hours of the night had accustomed her to surprises. Even so, she was taken aback by the sight of three men, bearing their luggage.

"The bad penny is back," Jeff said. "With a couple more just like it. I'm taking up the offer of staying in my old room, if it's still open."

"I been awake, waitin' you," Hettie said. "An' worryin'. I heard a lot of shootin'. Was you—"

"You can quit worrying," Jeff said. "It's all over. These are friends of mine who are in need of home-cooking, a kind word and a smile. Also a place to lay their weary heads."

Hettie glared at Clem and the Professor and sniffed disdainfully. Evidently word of their appearance in Wardrum was common knowledge.

"I ain't in the habit of standin' here in my wrapper to welcome company," Hettie said. "If they're hungry I'll get somethin' on the table as soon as possible."

The Professor took charge. "Jefferson put it crudely, ma'am," he said. "We desire only shelter and a place to sleep. We would not dream of imposing on you to any other extent at this hour."

"In the first place," Hettie said severely. "I ain't a ma'am. I wouldn't marry the best man alive. Even with the best you wouldn't get much."

"No man would be worthy," the Professor said. "That is self-evident."

"I've always heard you had a glib tongue," Hettie said.

"He can talk a clock into runnin' backwards, Miss," Clem stated. "If we're causin' any trouble we'll go away. Jeff, here, allowed that—"

"Who said anything about trouble?" Hettie snapped. "If Jefferson brought you, then you're more than welcome."

"This portly gentleman," Jeff said, "is Ephraim Kelso, as you evidently already know. The ugly one is Clement Devore."

"I've heard of both of you," Hettie said. "An' nothin' good."

"I feared as much," the Professor said sorrowfully. "Calumny, I assure you. Pure, outright falsehoods. Why, Clement and myself would not harm a—"

"Save your softsoap," Hettie sniffed. "I told you I ain't dressed proper to stand here listenin' to your blarney. I'll fetch some sandwiches an' pie an' coffee, an' get the beds ready. Leave your satchels here until I'm ready for them."

Jeff led the way to the kitchen where he got the stove started and made coffee.

"You called her Aunt," the Professor commented.

"Everybody in town does," Jeff said. "She and Alex were friends of my parents. They took me under their wing."

The Professor was silent for a time. "I knew your father," he said quietly. "And your mother."

Jeff was surprised. "You knew them?"

"Before even you were born," the Professor said. "At old Hays City back in Kansas in the trail-driving days. Your father was a deputy marshal, and I had come to Hays that summer as a young archeologist with an expedition that was fossil-hunting in the Smoky Hill country. Your mother was the daughter of homesteaders the Kansas Pacific Railroad brought into the country."

Jeff nodded. "She was a Zulu. That was in the days when they first started chalking that name on box cars."

"Nellie Jefferson was the prettiest girl in Kansas," the Professor said. "In the whole world as far as I was concerned. I was deeply in love with her." He was silent for a time. "I never got over it," he said. "But she picked the right man. Matt Temple."

Jeff was startled. Appalled. He understood he was being told why the Professor had become a drifter on the frontier. He saw Clem look at the Professor with understanding and compassion.

"Not long after Nellie and your father were married they left Hays," the Professor went on. "I learned later that they had settled in Wardrum. I met Matt some years afterward in Deadwood in the Dakota Black Hills."

"That was when he and Roosevelt became friends," Jeff said. "He went into Dakota on a gold stampede. He never found any gold. He was gone from Wardrum more than a year. I was about twelve then."

A new silence came. The Professor spoke. "I see pity for me in both you and Clement. That, I resent. I happen to prefer my way of life and the manner in which I earn my daily bread."

"Speakin' of daily bread," Clem said. "Let's take a look at some of it."

He drew from his pocket a billfold and opened it. He extracted four crisp, new fifty-dollar notes.

He eyed Jeff quizzically. "I reckon you know where I got these?"

Jeff nodded. "Camo money. Bill Hammond."

"To be exact, it was that taffy-haired secretary of his that handed it to me. A month's pay in advance. The Professor got the same."

He produced another banknote, also of fifty-dollar denomination. "This is the one the Professor saw me hold out of Reelfoot's wad."

He spread the bills on the table, weighing them flat with knives and forks.

"They look like they came from the same roost, don't they?" he asked.

Hettie entered the kitchen. She had donned a housedress and was tying on an apron. She halted, gazing at the three men who were so intent on the money on the table.

The Professor produced the banknotes he had flashed for Jeff's benefit in the Open Switch. He lined them alongside the others. "There's one missing," he said. "I spent it in the course of the evening."

The numbers on the bills that belonged to Clem and the Professor were consecutive, excepting the missing one the Professor had cashed.

There was a gap of only ten numbers between these and the bill Clem had taken from Reelfoot's funds.

Jeff frowningly studied the display. The Professor seemed sardonically amused, as though he was enjoying some bitter jest. Hettie remained silent in the background, fascinated by their expressions.

Clem poured coffee for all of them. He tested its temperature with his lips and recoiled, mumbling his grievance.

"It *could* be easy to explain," Jeff said. "There's little or no demand for bills of this size. They could have been handed out at the bank from the same packet to different persons. Days apart. Even weeks."

"Sure," Clem said. "Sure they could."

"Indubitably," the Professor murmured.

"All right," Jeff said. "So you don't believe that."

"Who possesses the missing ten bills?" the Professor asked.

"You tell me," Jeff said.

"At the going rate," Clem remarked, "that'd mean only two and a half men our size, Professor."

He added speculatively. "Come to think of it, I never yet had to go up against half a man. Wouldn't that be something to rattle your funny bone?"

Jeff heard a vehicle swing into the unpaved alley at the rear and turn into the stableyard. That would be Alex, arriving.

He left the kitchen by way of the rear door and met the buggy. Alex alighted and peered at him. "Why, hello, young man," he said gruffly. But there was a lift to his voice.

Jeff began helping unhitch the horse. "I'm taking up the offer to stay in my old room," he said. "And, if you don't mind, I've brought a couple of friends."

"Of course," Alex said.

He gripped Jeff by the arms, shook him affectionately. Jeff knew that all was right between them again. As right as it would ever be. Alex would never stop regretting that Jeff had abandoned doctoring, but he was reconciled to it.

"You looked fagged," Jeff said. "You've had more than that baby delivery tonight. I remember now that you left in that fellow's own rig."

"That was a false alarm again," Alex snorted. "Right after he brought me back I had another call. A freighter had a heart attack on the trail a couple of miles west of town. I got him back on his feet. It was on my way home that I ran into real grief. It was one of the Zulus."

"Zulus?"

"They intercepted me as I came into town. Somebody had shot a man in their camp. Bushwhacked him."

He eyed Jeff closely in the faint light. "There was a fight between the Zulus and the cattlemen while I was away on that call," he said slowly. "You know about that, of course."

"I know," Jeff said. "This Zulu—?"

"They told me he had been shot from a distance after it seemed the trouble was all over," Alex said. "Somebody out in the brush picked him off with a rifle. In the back. Lung wound. I worked on him, but I was too late. He only lasted a minute or two after I got there. He kept trying to say something, but I couldn't make out what it was."

Clem and the Professor had joined them and were listening.

Alex said futilely, "If I'd got there five minutes earlier there might have been a chance. They kept praying. They prayed so hard. They loved him. It's times like that when you wish you weren't a doctor. But I couldn't save him."

"Who prayed?" Jeff asked.

"His family. His wife and children. They had four young ones."

Jeff had to force himself to ask the next question. "What was the man's name?"

"Slocum," Alex said. "Ralph Slocum."

He looked at Jeff. "That's the father of the boy whose dog had the busted leg. He's . . ."

He quit talking. He did not understand the expressions of the three men.

"It's well started," Jeff said to Clem and the Professor. "That's three dead already."

# CHAPTER EIGHT

Because it was the Sabbath, Hettie rang the mealtime bell an hour later than usual the next morning. They sat down to a breakfast of steak and eggs flanked by plates of crisp biscuits and a choice of jellies and wild berry preserves.

"Miss, you make a man feel that startin' a new day is mighty worth while," Clem said.

"Every new day is worth while," Hettie said, and there was no bite to her tongue.

The Professor spoke, "If you will so permit, Doctor, it will be my humble privilege to thank the Lord this morning."

They bowed their heads and the Professor said, "Thank Thee, oh Lord, for this bounty Thou has provided. Guard those who partake of this goodness from all evil. Guide them from error in their own actions and judgment and advise them against wrong judgment of others. Guide and advise them in these things, for they are not sure of the way, nor of where they are traveling."

They joined in the "Amen." Jeff heard Clem speak with particular fervency.

There was a period of silence. Alex broke it, trying to be brisk. "Thank you, Mr. Kelso. Such a fine saying of grace is a good start to the day."

In all of them was the realization that the Professor's supplication had special significance. Where, Jeff asked himself, were they going and what was their destination?

A church bell began tolling in the town. That, Jeff remembered, would be the old log-built church on the west fringe of town that he had attended as a boy with his parents. Lila Mackay had said that she sang in the choir there.

"It'll be an hour before the service begins," Hettie said. She glared at them severely, giving the Professor particular attention. "If you ask me, listenin' to a little preachin' would do some of us a lot of good."

"No doubt," the Professor said. His mood remained deep and thoughtful—almost sad.

Jeff shared that heaviness of spirit. The feud that had been slowly growing was now out of hand. Up to a point, the opening of the Walking Hills had been a matter of rhetoric and political strategy.

It had reached a new basis. The physical element had taken over. A woman slain, a gunman dead. Ralph Slocum gone, paying with his life for killing the raider.

Or had it been only a matter of retaliation? Jeff was remembering that Ralph Slocum had said he could identify the man who had shot down Jennie Barnes.

Jeff thought of Lila's father, riding away into the darkness, alone and secretly. That must have been about the time Alex had been trying to save the life of Ralph Slocum in the Zulu camp.

Jeff had not mentioned having seen Peter Mackay riding out of town the previous night even to Clem or the Professor. And none of them had mentioned to Alex the coincidence of the serial numbers on the banknotes.

"Who's right?" Jeff suddenly asked.

Alex sighed. "They're both right and they're both wrong. That's why it's going to be so hard to stop it. There's no need for violence. It's as though both sides were possessed of some kind of a madness that keeps pushing them. Pushing them into bloodshed."

"What does Peter Mackay stand to lose if he's forced out of the Hills?"

"Lose? Why, about everything, I imagine. He's taken on a big bite. He's spread thin. Any sort of real bad luck will likely clean him out."

"Elucidate, sir," the Professor requested.

Alex laughed. "I haven't heard that word since I used it in college to impress a professor. He wasn't impressed. I *will* elucidate. Peter Mackay is an old mosshorn cattleman. He's Texas-born. He was a trail driver in his early days. He ranched in Texas but barbed wire and drought drove him out. He moved his brand to Colorado. He was sheeped out that time. He looked around, hunting a place where he would be at peace. He said he wanted a range where a cow could sneeze without some damned sodbuster suing him for bringing on pneumonia."

"And the Walking Hills filled the bill," Jeff commented.

"He knew he'd have to go big and figure on a thin margin of profit up here," Alex said. "He bought up half the claims that had been patented in the early days. He took over a couple of patched-saddle outfits that had water rights on the stream, based on homesteaded land. He went into black Angus cattle. They rustle well and stand the winters. They drop their calves without help. He's beginning to do better with his Angus than Tass Verity and others are with whitefaces."

"Buildin' up a new strain of beef takes hard work, luck and patience," Clem said. "An' a lot of cash."

"He's had to borrow money," Alex said.

"What about the rest of the outfits?" Jeff asked.

"Tass Verity's Block T is the only one that really counts, just as it did when you were riding for him," Alex said. "Tass is still on a sound footing. He's a hardheaded old cuss. The other brands are still small. They're only the tail to the kite. They stand to lose everything too, but Pete would get the worst jolt."

"And there's been no word where the President stands on this?"

"Not a word. Bill Hammond says Camo is sure to get the charter. I suppose he's right. After all, a railroad generally is a good thing for a country."

"But the President's been on the fence since you and the others went back there to see him?"

Alex nodded. "He listened mighty close to what we had to say."

"Then why have the cattlemen started this shooting?"

"That's the question," Alex sighed.

"They might have had things running their way at the White House. Don't they realize that what they're doing will turn a man like Roosevelt against them?"

"They ought to," Alex said. "The idiots!" He added grimly, "Worse than that, they're murderers. What's come over them?"

Aunt Hettie came hurrying in, clad in rustling silk, a prayer book in her hand. "I'm leaving," she said.

"If I miss church," Jeff said, "pray a little harder, to make up for it."

"I always pray hard and sing loud," Aunt Hettie said. "I want the good Lord to know I'm present."

After she had left, Jeff sat, mulling thoughts over. Presently, in the distance, he heard the organ in the church. The choir joined in, the sound faint and sweet in the quiet of the morning. He tried to imagine he could make out Lila Mackay's voice. The singing ended and he could picture the congregation settling down to listen to the preaching.

He arose. "I'm taking a little stroll."

"You should have company," the Professor said, glancing significantly at Jeff's side.

Jeff was unarmed. "You may be right, even on Sunday," he said. He got his holster and buckled it on.

Clem and the Professor followed him to the porch. "Any suggestions?" Clem asked.

"Just spend a quiet day at home."

Clem nodded. "Maybe you're right. It's best not to crowd them. From what the Doc tells me it don't look like Mackay or this Tass Verity are the kind who'll spook easy."

Jeff left them and walked into DeSmet Street. Cowponies and ranch vehicles crowded the space around the church some two blocks west.

Jeff could hear the voice of the preacher still sawing away. That soon ended and the congregation began uttering the closing prayer.

All activity in old town seemed concentrated at the church. The remainder of DeSmet Street was deserted. Every store was closed, the blinds drawn. Some had wooden shutters battened in place, relics of the old wild days when cowboys sometimes tried to tree the town. Now they were in use again.

New town was busy. Men were swarming near the Camo depot at the foot of DeSmet Street. Jeff saw that they were Zulus from the settlers' camp.

A black-plumed hearse, drawn by white horses, came into view and turned into DeSmet Street. It was followed by Ozzie Stone's secondary black, varnished wagon, which also bore mourning plumes. It was being used as a hearse for a double burial.

These vehicles were followed by two rented hackney coaches in which sat women and children—the families and close kin of Ralph Slocum and Jennie Barnes, no doubt.

The men formed into a military column, eight abreast, and swung into stride back of the carriages.

Files of eight men walked on each side of the hearses, acting as honor guards. All members wore mourning bands on their sleeves. Each man was armed. Among the rank and file were weapons also.

New arrivals appeared in DeSmet Street. Four men stepped into view not far from the church and took positions with their backs to a building. One was Arch Stanton. With him was Bass Brackett. The other two men were strangers to Jeff, but their earmarks were unmistakable. They were hired fighting men.

Fletch Jones and Red Kramer were absent, but Jeff had no doubt but that they were near, under cover, and perhaps with other gunmen at their side.

If the Zulus were aware of this display of fighting strength, they were not cowed. The funeral procession came steadily up DeSmet Street, advancing into the stronghold of the ranchers.

Jeff moved into the center of the street and walked closer to Stanton and his men. "What's your point, Arch?" he asked. "You might start hell popping."

"Let it pop," Stanton said.

In the church the organ struck up the recessional. The choir joined in. The service was ending.

Jeff turned and walked down the street to meet the oncoming cortege. The faces of the marching men were grim. They had seen the four waiting near the church.

Jeff stood in the path of the hearses. The driver of the leading vehicle said hoarsely, "Git out of the way, Mr. Temple."

"So you know me?" Jeff said. He caught the bridle of the near horse and forcibly halted the hearse. The procession came to a stop.

"There'll be more men coming out of that church in a minute," Jeff said. "They won't back down an inch."

"That's up to them, Mr. Temple," the driver said. He was a bearded man of fifty. Apparently he was looked on as the spokesman of the settlers. He had a Winchester rifle on the seat beside him, and a pistol was in his belt.

The driver added, "We want them cattlemen to see what they've done. We aim to have preachin' over Ralph Slocum an' Jennie Barnes right in their own damned church an' by their own damned preacher. Then we aim to take Ralph an' Jennie to their graveyard an' lay them to rest where the cowmen kin always have their tombstones to remember that they murdered them."

Jeff heard the chatter of voices up the street that told that the congregation was emerging from the church. The sound at first was the usual homely twittering and soft laughter of women greeting neighbors and friends. It changed to a sudden higher pitch, then died completely.

Without looking back Jeff knew that the increasing group in front of the church was standing staring at the somber procession that stood halted in the street.

There would be no stopping the settlers now. Not with their opponents watching.

Jeff accepted that fact. "There'll be no shooting," he said. "Nor a word from a one of you. I'll do all the talking. All of it, understand? I'll cut down the first man who makes a move toward his gun. You all seem to know me. Then you must also know that I'll do what I say."

He made sure his voice carried in the silence so that they heard him at the church. He spoke again. "That goes for either side."

He released his grip on the horses and motioned the driver to proceed. He turned and walked in the middle of the street, leading the way. The honor guard swung into step. The cortege got into motion.

Jeff could see the cattlemen ordering their women and children to move away. The majority of them were obeying but several of the women remained where they were.

The centerpoint of this refusal was Lila Mackay. She wore a summery dress and a bonnet and had a white hymnbook under her arm. She stood at the side of Aunt Hettie Crabtree who was also scorning appeals to scurry to safety.

The men around them were donning holsters or loading rifles that they had seized up from saddles and vehicles.

Jeff continued marching ahead. He was now the one who set the pace for the cortege. Only Lila Mackay's face stood out from the others for him as he came nearer.

She was pale. She was gazing at him and there were many emotions in her eyes. Above all was a protest and a question. She was asking him why? Why was he taking up sides against her father?

But above all, there was abandonment in her expression. It seemed to him that she was abandoning new dreams, putting new desires out of her mind. He could understand how dreary her thoughts might be, for they matched the emptiness in his own mind.

He lifted his hand and halted the cortege in front of the church. He faced bleak, bitter eyes. Evans Johnson was there. And Dan Mulhall. And many others with whom he had ridden and been friends in the past. Owners and riders. All of Walking Hills had turned out on this Sunday as though the word of a showdown had been passed around.

Jeff spoke. "All that's wanted is the church in which to let the coffins stand for awhile. And for the minister to say a prayer over what's mortal of Ralph Slocum and Jennie Barnes, and then to bury them in ground that's reserved for the peace of the dead."

Nobody spoke for a throbbing space of time. Jeff could

see the anger in the faces of the ranchers. To them the request was an insult.

The moment lengthened. Jeff expected that some hothead would touch off the explosion by going for his gun.

It was Evans Johnson who made the decision against gunplay. His seamy face was gray and hard. Jeff could see that he bowed to necessity only at bitter cost to his pride.

"We bar no man or woman, dead or alive, from this church of God," Johnson said harshly.

It seemed that everyone began breathing again. So close had many been to death, so narrow had been the escape.

Jeff nodded to the cortege. Files of settlers lifted the plain wooden boxes from the vehicles and carried them on their shoulders into the church, passing the ranch people who had drawn grimly together. Other Zulus, carrying picks and shovels, continued on up the street toward the burial ground to dig the graves.

Jeff saw that this was only a truce. He had forced it on them. He looked at Lila. She was empty of emotion. She showed no anger, no reproach. That made it all the more hopeless. She turned away.

Her example was followed by the others. The ranchers and their families moved to the waiting horses and vehicles. Cinches were tightened and women and children were helped into buckwagons and buggies. Wheels creaked, saddle leather squeaked, and they began streaming out of town, heading back to the Walking Hills.

Lila and Aunt Hettie walked down the street. Lila halted at a corner and kissed Aunt Hettie on the cheek. They parted, Lila continuing on to the hotel while Aunt Hettie turned homeward, her back straight as a ramrod.

Four riders waited near the livery. A buckwagon, loaded with supplies, appeared from the livery barn, driven by a wrinkled Chinese. The cook at the Mackay place, Jeff surmised.

Presently, Lila came from the hotel, carrying the bundles she had acquired in her Saturday shopping. She joined the riders, mounted sidesaddle and rode away, armed cowboys at her side. She looked at Jeff as she passed by and said, "Good-by."

Jeff discovered that the Professor and Clem were standing in a doorway nearby. Clem was chewing on a strand of grass. The Professor had his plug hat tipped back and seemed lost in thought. Both carried braces of six-shooters. Jeff knew that they must have been there from the start.

Arch Stanton and his men had vanished. Except for a cluster of settlers around the door of the church, which could not accommodate them all, there were no other persons in sight.

He had the sensation of standing on a deserted battlefield from which the armies had backed off without settling the issue. He was a ghost and so was the Professor and so was Clem. He had been left alone with his own kind, with the embodiment of men whose lives were in the past and who knew they were living on borrowed time.

Clem flipped away the stem of grass. The Professor straightened his hat. They eyed Jeff inquiringly, but he had no word for them, so they headed back down the side street toward the Crabtree residence.

Presently the services in the church ended. The coffins were carried back to the carriage. The funeral cortege formed again and moved on westward out of town toward the graveyard. DeSmet Street was now completely deserted, except for himself.

He turned and walked down the street, heading for the jail to see Ramon Montez and tell him that things seemed to be working out all right. At least for Ramon.

## CHAPTER NINE

Jeff returned to the Crabtree house and found Alex and the Professor squabbling noisily over a checker game.

"I've got a yearning for a taste of pheasant," he said. "If you can fix me up with a bird gun, a saddle horse and a camp pack, Alex, I'll go down along the Little Beaver."

"Help yourself," Alex said. "You know where to find my stuff. It's where it's always been."

"I'll camp overnight," Jeff said. "I'll stop by Ramon's place on the way and talk to Dolores."

The truth was that he knew the Mackay ranch lay in that direction. Within him was the longing to talk to Lila Mackay again. Maybe to explain. At least to see her.

In addition, he had to get away from Wardrum and its bitterness for awhile and try to think this out. The murder of Jennie Barnes had been brutal enough, but it could have been the unpremeditated act of a panicky man. Even so, the frontier code was unyielding where protection of women was concerned. The killer stood a good chance of being lynched if caught.

Worse, in some respects, had been the murder of Ralph Slocum. That had been a coldly-calculated act of self-protection.

He kept remembering Peter Mackay riding secretly out of town into the darkness at the time Slocum lay dying.

He was soon mounted, with his camp pack lashed down. Alex owned a good roan saddle horse in addition to harness animals, and Aunt Hettie had furnished him with what he needed in cooking equipment. Alex and the Professor were still engrossed in their combat at the checker table on the porch. Clem was writing a letter. To his wife, Jeff surmised.

"I'll stop by the Zulu camp on my way and take a look at that pothound's leg," Jeff said.

"You might inquire around," Alex said. "If any of those people are ailing I'd appreciate it if you'd take a look at them."

Jeff eyed him closer. "Anything special on your mind?"

"Most anything could break out, the way they're living, all bunched up," Alex said.

"Anything definite?"

"No," Alex said. "We've had a scare or two. Ken Saunders—that's one of the other sawbones in town—thought he might have had smallpox on his hands a few days ago, but it turned out that the child only had a rash. Ken and Joe Dittman and myself are keeping our fingers crossed. Joe's the other doctor."

"All right," Jeff said. "If I notice anything I'll come back."

He rode across the tracks into the settlers' camp. It was like entering a besieged, armed village. The Zulus were under a strain, and jumpy. It was apparent they believed they were in for more trouble. It was also plain that they were braced to meet it.

Some of the younger men came hurrying to crowd around. Their curiosity was annoying. The older men seemed more reserved, neither friendly nor hostile. Jeff guessed that Bill Hammond had assured them that they would have help if it came to gun trouble and that Jeff Temple would be one of those who did the helping.

"I came to take a look at Chub Slocum's dog," he said.

The man who had been driving the hearse the previous day moved to the front. "I'm Homer Craig," he said.

He led Jeff to where the muzzled patient lay. The Slocum family was absent. "Angie an' her brood took some wildflowers to the grave," Homer Craig explained. "I reckon they'll stay there with Ralph for awhile. Angie can't make herself believe he's gone."

The dog, which lay on a straw pallet, greeted Jeff with an attempt at tail-thumping. Jeff examined the splinted leg and nodded. He was satisfied with his handiwork. "Tell Chub that old Prince is doing fine and might be back on his feet in a week or so," he said. "I'll give the word when it comes time to take off the splints."

He looked around. "Is anybody under the weather in camp?"

"There sure is," Homer Craig said glumly. "Lots o' folks air ailin'. I sure ain't feelin' none too chipper myself."

"What's wrong?"

"It's that dratted lumbago," Craig complained. "It comes back on me right smart every time I go an' get myself all worked up, such as lately."

"What about the others?"

The other ailing Zulus, like Homer Craig, had chronic afflictions that were mainly subjects of conversation and much treasured by their possessors. Jeff spent half an hour visiting the ones Craig named. They required little more than a wise look and a sympathetic ear into which to pour their stories of troubles that were mainly fancied.

Jeff finished with the sick list and prepared to mount. "If anybody else gets to ailing," he told Homer Craig, "*really* ailing, I mean, send for Dr. Crabtree or one of the other doctors at once."

He hesitated. "If they're not around and I happen to be handy I'll come and take a look."

He rode away, deriding himself for being dramatic. Alex had baited a trap for him and he had stepped into it. He had enjoyed that little bout with the chronic sufferers. Imaginary ills were as much a part of a doctor's life as genuine maladies.

The Zulus were susceptible to epidemics, of course, because of the makeshift conditions under which they were living, but, knowing Alex, Jeff was sure that he and the other medical men were very much alive to the danger and were prepared to act in a hurry if the need came. By this little bit of adroitness, Alex had drawn Jeff into his medical clique and had placed some of the responsibility on his shoulders.

Jeff rode past the hayfields beyond the creek. Presently he turned off the main trail down a ranch road which led for a hot mile through sagebrush, then descended into a flat along Wardrum Creek and into the yard of a small ranch. The buildings were log-built, with sod roofs. The place was surrounded by fields of ripe, uncut hay.

Two children who had been playing in the yard ran excitedly to the house. A comely, dark-haired young woman appeared in the door, a hand shading her eyes.

She came hurrying into the open yard, her eyes widening. "Madre Dios!" she cried. "It *is* you! It is! It is!"

Jeff dismounted and kissed her on the cheek. She was the wife of Ramon Montez. Like Ramon, she was a native of Argentina, but she had been one of the *genta fina,* the fine people, a member of the wealthy aristocracy of the *rancheros*. She must have been very young when she had eloped with Ramon, for she was still young and vivacious, but he could see that this was now darkened by fear and anxiety.

"The *ninos* are *ninos* no longer," Jeff said, grinning at the children who were hovering shyly in the background. "It's three years since I've seen them. So what? Young Ramon looks like he's about to grow as tall as his father. Juanita is threatening to turn out to be prettier than even you, Dolores. There'll be many a heart broken by that one."

Dolores' eyes kept searching his face, asking an urgent question. He nodded and said, "Ramon should be home soon. Maybe tomorrow."

Her hands went to her eyes to hide her tears. "Just like that!" she sobbed. "So it is all over? After all these days of eating my heart out, you come home and—poof! It is settled so quickly. Oh, Jeef, Jeef! How did you bring this thing about? Why did they do this thing to my Ramon? My poor, little, innocent dove. My hoosband."

Jeff laughed. "He might be your little dove, but to me, this hoosband of yours stacks up at about two hundred pounds on the hoof and six feet of whang leather and bullhide. Anyway you should soon have him back on your hands to fuss over."

Her joy subsided. "Then it is not certain that he will be freed?" she breathed. "It is not really settled?"

"I'm ninety percent sure," Jeff said.

"They have not admitted that this charge is a big, terrible lie? A—a—what do you call it—a frame-down?"

"Frame-up," Jeff said. He debated his answer a moment. "I have the word of the general manager of Camo that the charges will be dropped. It'll take a little time, perhaps."

"I will wait," Dolores said tragically. "I will wait."

Dolores had always been dramatic. And she had always been supremely loyal to Ramon. And supremely happy. If she had ever regretted having given up the sheltered life of her birthright when she had fallen in love with the handsome *vaquero* who had worked on her father's *rancho,* she had never let it cloud her life with Ramon.

Jeff had never asked these two why they had exiled themselves to the plains of North America. Ramon had mentioned once, briefly, that it had been a revolution against the politicians, against corruption and thievery in high places, and that he had been one of those who had led the cause and had lost. He had been arrayed against the *genta fina,* which meant that he had opposed the aristocracy. There had also been a duel that was not over politics, but because of Dolores.

"With *pistolas,"* Ramon had said. "He was an important man among the politicos. I had to leave the Argentine. Dolores came with me."

Jeff gave each of the children a silver dollar. He kissed Dolores again on the cheek.

"You must not leave so soon!" she protested. "We must talk. It has been so long, Jeef."

"Another day," Jeff said. "When Ramon comes back. We'll talk. We'll drink. Today is my thinking day. I've got a few problems to wrangle with."

Dolores understood. "I have always believed it is a fine thing for one to come back to the place where they were born," she said.

"You haven't forgotten the Argentine, have you, Dolores?" Jeff said gently.

"No," she said. "No I have not. But it was not that I was thinking about. We will never go back to the Argentine. Ramon and myself are happy here in this country. But it is you I am worrying about."

"Worrying?"

"I know there is much that is going on in this country, these Walking Hills, that is not good. Much that nobody understands. I know why it was to Ramon that this thing happened. Do you know this too, Jeef?"

When he didn't speak she supplied the answer. "To bring you back here to get—what you call it—scrambled up in this trouble that is coming."

"Now why did you ever get any idea like that?"

"Because I know you. Because I knew your good father and your sweet mother. Because the name of Temple is a fine name in this country. A proud name. One that people look up to."

She added, "They are using Ramon to force you to do things you have no wish to do."

Jeff tried to laugh at her fears. "Nobody can force me to get scrambled up in anything I don't want to mix into. I'm a grown man with my eyes open."

"I will pray for you," Dolores said. "I will pray for you and Ramon."

"He'll be back in time to take in that hay before it mildews," Jeff said. "I'll come out and give him a hand. I haven't stacked hay in years."

But the worry was back with Dolores as she watched him ride away. At least it was no longer the lost hope that had burdened her previously.

He rode southward. The sagebrush plain rose in an enormous swell for some two or three miles, so imperceptibly there was no sensation of climbing until the crest was reached. And at the summit there was no summit. Only a vista of other swales and summits ahead that, like this one, no man was ever sure he had reached.

It was a stupendous sweep of land that undulated into the vastness until it merged with the low-lying purple shadow on the horizon that was the Grindstone Mountains eighty miles away. Only the golden bloom of the rabbit brush gave tone to the gray-green loneliness.

These were the Walking Hills.

Far to the west and south Jeff could make out the buildings of Tass Verity's Block T headquarters, where he had worked roundup during beef gather on two occasions when home from medical school. The Block T lay cradled in the notch below wrinkled bluffs from whose base a live spring flowed to form the main source of the Little Beaver.

He rode farther into the Walking Hills. The wagon trail that he followed presently joined the route of a twin line of surveyors' stakes. This could only be Camo's right-of-way southward. The stakes marched in a ruler-straight column through the heart of the Walking Hills.

He sighted range cattle, their numbers thin amid the immensity of the land. Some of them were black Angus —Mackay cattle, and they were in good flesh and evidently thriving.

The thin, brushy course of the Little Beaver slowly emerged in view far ahead, disappearing into the sagebrush and reappearing as he followed the roll of the swells.

He sighted the buildings of another ranch, beyond the stream. It had not been there when he had last ridden down this trail. That would be the Mackay Rocking PM headquarters. It was flanked by fenced hayfields. That too vanished from view as he descended imperceptibly into the mighty swale that cupped the Little Beaver.

Familiar scenes came rising to meet him. He was riding through a land rich in memories. Here was the draw where he had shot a loafer wolf and had collected ten dollars bounty from the cattle association. He had been bursting with pride, for he had been only eleven years old at the time and it was the first real money he had earned.

He remembered how his mother had sighed. He hadn't understood that at the time. He did now. Nellie Temple had been confronted at that moment by the realization that all mothers inevitably face when they discover that their offspring was taking the responsibilities of life into his own hand.

He recalled the quiet grin on his father's face. "A neat shot," had been Matt Temple's only comment. He had added, later on, "Come first heavy frost, we'll go down to the Grindstones and see if you can't get yourself a nice, young, fat elk. We need meat for winter and it's time you helped with the hunting."

This ride through the past was peace. This was contentment. Wardrum and its hatreds seemed far, far away, lost in the run of the hills that now rose mysteriously on his backtrail, although he did not remember crossing hills.

Here, by this big white boulder, was where the Temples had often nooned to eat the cold chicken and potato salad and cake from the picnic basket while they were on their way on camping trips to the Grindstones, or en route to the marshes along the Little Beaver to bag mallard and a wild goose or two and to gather the ripe wild plums for jam and jelly. He had been seven in those days. Eight. Nine. He remembered the trout they cooked that he had caught in Little Beaver, using a scrap of red calico from his mother's sewing bag as a lure. They had lived. They had laughed.

He had been nineteen the last time he had ridden on a hunting trip down this trail with his father. In the swale past which he was now jogging, where the sage grew to the stirrup, they had seen a buffalo—an unbelievable trophy—for it had been accepted that buffalo had been extinct in the Walking Hills for fifteen years or more.

Neither he nor his father had made a move to lift their rifles. They had sat in the saddle, gazing. Matt Temple had been a handsome man. Straight-shouldered, soft-spoken, with thick dark hair and understanding dark eyes.

Jeff recalled the look that had been on his father's face that day. Tender, wistful, reminiscent. Matt Temple, as a young man, had seen the buffalo herds carpet the plains.

They had sat watching the lone bull until it had grazed out of sight, swallowed by the gray-green Walking Hills.

"An old bull, gray as the rocks of the Grindstones," Matt Temple had said softly. "That must be where he came from. He likely was born and lived out his life in some basin there that hunters never found."

He had added, "He's come out onto the plains to die. Never tell anyone about this, Jeff. They'd hunt him down. Let's not be his executioners."

That had been a magic day. They had come upon elk in bands of a size Jeff had never seen before or since. They had flushed quail and pheasant by the thousands. Sage hens had been almost underfoot in the path of the horses. They had listened to wild sounds in the sky. "Trumpeter swans," Matt Temple had said. "Flying south. A royal bird."

They had not fired a shot that day. It had been their last ride together and it was as though nature wanted to show to them its complete beauty.

Not long afterward Jeff had left to begin his seven years of college and medical schooling. His visits home had been sketchy, for he had usually hired out with one of the ranches as a rider to earn money to pay for his schooling.

Now his father was gone. His mother was gone. He came back to reality. The day was flawed, the land was lonely. Inevitably, down the trail he was riding, there would someday be a bullet in the back for him. Just as there had been one for Matt Temple. Just as there probably would be one for the Professor, and one for Clem Devore. Men who walked alone and made enemies of violent persons.

At least, Jeff reflected, there would be no one to take the bullet that was meant for him—no woman to die as his mother did and leave him with searing regrets. There would be no flesh except his own to be torn by the guns of vengeance, such as Clem's wife.

The wagontrack thread through the vastness of the Hills carried him onward with his memories. The sun was swinging low. A cooling wind rustled in the sage. Dust devils held their dance on a cleared flat where some early-day settler had grubbed out the sagebrush and had tried to dry-farm. Tumbleweeds found foothold there. He sighted other such clearings. The cabins those forgotten pioneers had built were tumble-down ruins now, their logs serving as fuel for the campfires of line riders and roundup wagons.

Some of those logs had bullet holes and even war arrowheads buried in them, for this land had been first settled in the days when the plains Indians were riding. Settled, abandoned, and finally given over to the cattlemen. To tough men and to tough breeds of animals, for only cattle that could rustle on flinty land and range twenty miles from water could survive in the Walking Hills.

Now the homesteading was to be tried again by the Zulus. More dusty flats would appear in the sage, more cabins would be raised. There would eventually be more dust devils dancing over the ruins of men's backbreaking attempts to buck nature's odds.

And Jeff was bound to their chariot, obligated to protect them and see to it that they got their chance to starve.

Far west of him and to the north, he picked up the dust of riders. They were lost among the swells for a long time. When he picked them up again, they had moved almost directly west. They were riding steadily.

He could not make out much about them, but he had an impression that one at least was a man as big as Bass Brackett. They seemed to be heading for Tass Verity's place. He studied them whenever the chance came, which was none too often, for they seemed to be making an effort to stay off the skyline. They were following no trail, but were keeping to the sagebrush.

He became sure the bulky one was Brackett. That meant the others were probably members of Arch Stanton's crew also. However, as he watched, he was convinced that none of the group resembled Stanton.

Finally the five, for he had counted their numbers by

that time, did not reappear again. They had either halted, or were following a draw that concealed them.

He rode onward, for the sun was low. It was still good shooting light when he came to the Little Beaver. Pheasants were coming in for water and he soon had a brace.

He pitched camp, dressed the birds and hung them to cool. He ignited a fire, and while it was burning down to hot coals, he stripped and dove into a rocky pool in the stream. It was where he had swum as a boy. At least this had not changed. He shouted aloud as the shock of the chill water drove through him. He emerged, tingling, dried himself and dressed.

While the pheasants were cooking he opened a can of tomatoes and set the coffeepot to boil. He speared the golden-brown delicacies from the skillet and ate with keen relish.

He finished off with a can of peaches. He was still working on the peaches when he heard a horse coming fast. The trail was within shouting distance and his campfire was visible. The rider swung off the trail and came crashing through the sagebrush and among the willows to the sandy clearing where the beacon burned.

Jeff moved back so that he would not be outlined against the fire, and made sure his pistol was loose in the holster.

The arrival was Lila Mackay. She was astride in a divided skirt, boots and a plaid waist and duck vest, with a white scarf tied around her hair. She alighted in the firelight.

She was under strain. Jeff walked back into the light. She understood that he had been braced for gun trouble. She said, "I should have known better than to come into a night camp without calling out. I forgot my manners. But I'm worried. It's my father! He's hurt! He needs a doctor."

"What's wrong?"

"He accidentally shot himself while he was cleaning his rifle last night. He was foolish enough to believe it wouldn't amount to much. He poured some whisky on it, and tied it up and didn't say anything about it to anyone. His arm is frightfully swollen."

"His arm?" Jeff asked.

"Yes. I'm afraid the bullet's still in it. It's his left arm."

# CHAPTER TEN

Lila stood gazing at him, puzzled by his expression. He was telling himself that she didn't know that the man who had killed Jennie Barnes in the raid on the Zulu camp had been shot in the left arm.

"Dad's in terrible pain," she spoke. "He needs attention. Fast. Will you come?"

"Alex Crabtree—" Jeff began.

"I've already sent a rider to town to fetch him. But that will take hours. And Doc Crabb might be away on a call. The other doctors might be out of reach too."

"I'll do what I can, of course," Jeff said.

Moving fast, he broke camp and saddled while Lila took care of dousing the fire.

"How far is it to your place?" he asked as they mounted.

"Not much more than a mile," she said. "You're on some of our land right now, as a matter of fact. All the frontage on the creek was homesteaded years ago and proved up. We've bought all we could get title to."

She sensed his next question and answered it before it was voiced. "You'd have come in sight of our ranch if you'd crossed the creek and ridden clear of the brush. I spotted you before sundown, riding up the trail."

"Spotted me?"

"There've been a lot of strangers drifting around the country lately. We've got binoculars mounted on a platform in a big cottonwood in the yard. The tree is high enough so that we can get a look-see for quite a distance in all directions without anyone knowing they're being watched."

"These strangers?" Jeff asked. "What kind of earmarks do they have?"

"A lot of them are Zulus, of course, sizing up the country or hunting game. But Camo had some pretty questionable characters on their survey crews and working with their drilling outfits."

"I rate as one of these questionable galoots, of course," Jeff observed. "How long was I under observation?"

"For quite some time," she confessed. "Snoopy, wasn't it?"

"I'll stay off the skylines after this," Jeff said, thinking of the riders he had sighted during the afternoon.

"I knew you had camped when you didn't show up south of the creek," she said. "I heard you shooting. It was about that time that I found out Dad had been hurt. He looked so pale I finally forced it out of him. He collapsed about then. I sent a man to Wardrum, then put him to bed and came to find you."

They came into view of the lights of a ranch and presently rode into a sizable spread. The buildings were of lodgepole pines that must have been freighted from the Grindstones. These were comparatively new in contrast to the age of the average ranch house in the country.

The main house was low and long. Peter Mackay had conformed to his Texas heritage in its planning. Its shake roof extended over an open gallery that ran the length of its west face. The doors of all the rooms opened on the gallery, which was floored with big red square tiles in the Spanish style.

Corrals, barns and haystacks loomed in the background along with the usual collection of mowing machines, rakes and stackers. The Rocking PM evidently was in the midst of mowing, for there were four men grouped on the benches alongside the bunkhouse door who were hayhands by their garb, members of the clan of itinerants who followed the harvests.

A chuckwagon stood in the open near the barn, fitted with a new white canvas top, one wheel on a jack. It was in the process of being placed in top condition for the beef gather that would be starting soon in the Walking Hills.

Four riders had been heelsquatting on the gallery of the main house, the tips of their cigarets glowing. They came to take care of the horses, but they did not speak as Jeff and Lila alighted.

In the lamplight from the windows, Jeff recognized two of them as men he had ridden with on roundups. They only nodded curtly in acknowledgment when he looked at them. They were hostile. They had him pegged as a friend no longer, but an opponent.

Lila led him down the gallery to an open door. "Father!" she called. "The doctor's here."

They stepped into a bedroom. Peter Mackay lay on the bed, bootless and bare to the waist. His left arm was covered by the sheet. His skin was the hue of slate. He lifted his head, his eyes sunken, bloodshot.

He glared at Jeff. "You?" He turned his gaze on Lila. "What's this man doing here?"

"I asked him to help you until Doc Crabb gets here," she said. "He was kind enough to come and try to do what he can."

"He's workin' for Bill Hammond," Mackay rasped.

"He can help you, Dad," she said. "He's a doctor."

Mackay looked at Jeff. "Doctor? You? I've heard it different. I don't ask any favors from you, Temple. Nor Bill Hammond."

Jeff moved to the bed. "Let's take a look at that arm," he said.

"Arm?" Mackay repeated. "There's nothing wrong with my arm. It's just a touch of malaria. Comes back on me every—"

He saw the expression in Jeff's face. His gaze swung wildly to Lila. He tried to voice a question, but all that came was incoherent mumbling. His head sank back on the pillow.

Jeff lifted the sheet from his arm. It bore a fresh bandage, but it was frightfully swollen and inflamed.

"Fetch warm water, a sharp scissors and clean cloths," he said.

Lila went hurrying to obey. Jeff shed his saddle jacket. Then he stripped off his shirt. He unbuckled his gunbelt and hung it on a chair.

He threw open the doors that led to other rooms, and opened a window that helped ventilate the room. He spoke to the riders who were waiting on the gallery. "I'll need every lamp in the place for light. Then get blankets and use them as fans to keep air moving through this room. This man is on fire with fever."

Using scissors and the warm water that Lila brought, he loosened the stiffened bandage from Peter Mackay's arm. It was swollen and discolored.

Lila's face turned a sickly hue. She swayed and clutched at a chair for support. Jeff caught her by the shoulders, shaking her. "Are you going to cave in every time you're needed?" he demanded roughly.

Resentment was a strong tonic. She pushed his hands away. "I won't keel over," she said, her lips stiff, her voice high-pitched. "That's a promise."

"If there's a medical kit, I can use it," Jeff said. "The bullet seems to still be in there, sure enough. It's got to come out. It's what's causing the trouble. The sooner we get at it the better."

He scowled at her. "And better have smelling salts handy if there's any around," he added. "Just in case."

She brought what medical equipment they had. This included a wealth of patent medicines, nostrums, salves and cure-all liniments and instruments that were for use on livestock. However, at least there was a probe that evidently had never been taken from its case, and carbolic and even a vial of chloroform, along with a sponge and a hood and a syringe.

"Fetch in a table," Jeff called to the riders. "A big one, if possible."

The table was provided, a huge, heavy, solid family heirloom with elaborately carved legs. It probably had been brought from Texas.

Lila covered it with sheets. Jeff, with the help of the men, lifted the patient on the operating table. Mackay lay in a daze and Jeff decided that the chloroform would not be necessary.

One of the men provided a razor which Jeff used as a scalpel. He swiftly drained off a flood of corruption from the inflamed arm. Lila again went ashen but she set her teeth and fought off nausea. One of the riders who had volunteered to stand by rushed out of the room, retching.

The bullet was imbedded above the elbow. The bone was damaged but not broken. Jeff worked speedily. Peter Mackay began to moan. He suddenly uttered a strangled gasp and went limp. He was bathed in icy sweat.

Jeff tossed on the table the bullet that he had extracted. "Quick!" he said. "A warm cloth on his head. Not a cold one. It's shock we're fighting now."

He worked desperately to strengthen respiration. He and Lila chafed legs and Mackay's right arm. Jeff feared that Mackay's heart was never going to rally from the shock of the probe.

At last the tide turned. Mackay's unsteady breathing settled down. The fluttering pulse suddenly became a trip-hammer beat. This gradually eased as they continued to work. The breathing strengthened. Finally, Jeff was able to apply a bandage to the arm. The patient was responding well.

He straightened. The riders were flapping blankets with desperate energy outside the room, keeping the air moving. They had pressed the haying crew into service.

Jeff tried to laugh. It was a croak. "You're going to huff and puff until you blow the damned house down," he said. "You can take it easier now."

He walked outside. One of the riders peered close at him, then rolled a cigaret and handed it to him. Lila held the match that lighted it.

She stood waiting. Jeff drew on the cigaret for a time, then finally answered her unspoken question. "I don't know yet. We'll have to wait awhile."

"Blood poisonin'?" a rider asked in a hushed voice.

The classical terms leaped into Jeff's mind. Severe phlegmon of the upper arm, with the beginning of lymphangitis. How easy it was to remember!

"Blood poisoning," he agreed.

He finished the cigaret and returned to the side of his patient. It was another half an hour before he straightened again.

"We may have got to it in time," he said. "I believe he's got a good chance of making it now."

He hesitated, then added, "I'm not sure about the arm. I'm afraid we'll have to take it."

"If only he lives," Lila said, "I'll thank God." She added, "And you."

Anger rose in Jeff. She saw it in his eyes and straightened, awaiting the storm.

He was wet with perspiration. He sponged his face and body in cool water that she brought. She handed him a towel. He scrubbed himself dry and donned his shirt. He buckled on the gunbelt.

"Never compare a doctor to God," he said. "I can tell you there's nothing holy about their work. They're butchers."

"I can't believe that," she said.

"They save the ones that should be left to die. They can't help the ones who ought to be allowed to live."

"Are you saying that my father doesn't deserve to live?"

"There are worse ways of dying," he said.

She was shaken. Her lips were ashen. "Exactly what do you mean by that?" she demanded.

How could he go about telling her that if he had saved Peter Mackay's life it was probably only a reprieve until the patient was brought to account for the murder of Jennie Barnes and the bushwhacking of Ralph Slocum?

He was spared that ordeal. A bullet smashed into the log walls of the house with an impact that jarred dust from the beams, causing the oil lamps to waver.

More bullets beat at the house. Wild yelling arose, along with the thud of galloping hoofs. Riders swept past the building, shooting and screeching.

Lila stood, frozen by fright, staring through the open door into the darkness where the guns were flaming. Jeff seized her and forced her to take shelter beneath the table. He lifted Mackay to the floor.

He leaped to extinguish the lamps. A waning moon had cleared the rim of the hills. In that faint light he saw the hooded rider who had jerked his horse to a halt in the ranch yard.

The masked man fired twice. Jeff felt the hot sting of the first bullet as it brushed his hair. The second slug missed only by a thin margin.

Up to that moment the raid had been only to terrorize—a thing of uproar and screeching, with the bullets meant only for the walls. It was a gesture of reprisal by the Zulus, no doubt, for the raid on their camp.

They had not been shooting to avenge Ralph Slocum and Jennie Barnes in blood at least. But these two bullets had been fired to kill. And Jeff had been their target.

His reaction was defensive. It was the instinctive, violent lashback of any trapped creature. He whirled and snatched his pistol from the holster and opened up.

The masked rider had wheeled his horse, using spurs to escape. Bullets struck him with savage force. Jeff saw the man slump in the saddle and hang on as his horse lunged out of the ranch yard and through the open wagon gate that led to the hayfield east of the house. Then he fell.

Two of the Mackay riders were shooting back now, firing from the bunkhouse which they had reached by risking a rush across the open yard. The other two cattle hands were flattened on the gallery, not daring to move, and swearing in bitter helplessness. Their guns were also in the bunkhouse. They could only hug the tiles and wait.

The raid concentrated at the rear of the house. Jeff extinguished the lamps and raced into an adjoining room. He stumbled over a chair in the darkness, collided with some other article of furniture and reached a window.

The barn and a wagonshed loomed blackly against the moonlight. He sighted two or three men on foot, retreating among the outbuildings. Like the masked rider he had traded shots with, they wore gunnysacks over their heads and shoulders.

He became aware of fire. Flames were rising overhead. The shake roof of the house was burning. The shooting at the front of the house had been a ruse to hold attention there while raiders on foot had slipped in at the rear and had tossed firewads on the roof.

Rifles opened up again on three sides, the bullets slamming into the walls. Lila came crawling to join him.

"The house is on fire!" she screamed.

"You can build a new house," Jeff said. "Keep your head down."

Rifles continued to pour bullets into the house. Jeff decided, despite the roar of shots, that there were no more than half a dozen men in on the raid. They were trying to give the impression of greater numbers.

The shooting abruptly tapered off and stopped. Someone had been sounding a shrilly whistled order. A moment later the pound of hoofs arose beyond the buildings and receded in the darkness.

It was over. The attackers had kept the Mackay contingent pinned down until the fire had gained headway on the roof.

Jeff ran outside. The whole thing had been so carefully planned and efficiently carried out that it had lasted scarcely more than five minutes. But the house was beyond saving. Flames were leaping a dozen feet in the air from the roof, and beginning to roar. A burning fireball, one of those the raiders had used, had rolled to the ground and lay flaming nearby. It was the oily waste from railroad cars. The same type of fireball the raiders had used on the Zulu camp.

Jeff and the cowboys carried Peter Mackay out of the house on a blanket and placed him in a bed in the bunkhouse. Jeff raced back and helped Lila, who was salvaging what valuables she could. The house was burning from end to end now. He finally refused to let her enter the structure again.

"The roof is about to cave in," he said.

The wind drove flying brands upon the barn and bunkhouse, and sparks threatened the haystacks near the corral. They all pitched in, forming a bucket line from the irrigation ditch that served the east hayfield. They worked desperately. It was touch and go for a time. Eventually the full fury of the flames from the house was spent and the danger to the other buildings faded.

Jeff walked to the bunkhouse. Lila, who had also helped in the bucket line, had preceded him, and was with her father. Peter Mackay was conscious. He was in pain, but he was strengthening.

He lifted his head. "How much is your fee, Temple?" he demanded, his voice faint.

"No, Dad!" Lila protested.

"How much?" Mackay croaked. "I didn't ask him to come here. If I'd had my say, I'd have waited for Crabtree. But I'll pay him, whatever the price."

"You don't owe me anything, Mackay," Jeff said. "I'm not a doctor. Maybe you'd have been better off in the long run if I'd let you alone."

Their eyes met. Peter Mackay understood what he meant. But Mackay's haggard eyes were only scornful. "Give him a gold piece," he said. "Ten dollars, Lila. Make it in silver. Ten pieces of silver. He isn't even worth the thirty they paid Judas. He's turned against his own kind of people."

"He saved your life," Lila said. "I brought him here. You're not being fair."

Her father ignored her. "Maybe I'm not offering enough. Maybe it isn't a doctor's fee he wants. That's small change in his line of work. Maybe it's real money he's after."

"Something in the way of a bribe?" Jeff asked icily.

"Money buys your guns, Temple," Mackay said. "It can buy anything from you, I reckon."

"You don't really imagine that money can keep this quiet, do you?" Jeff asked.

"What's your price, killer?" Mackay jeered.

"Every rider on the place tonight knows you've been carrying a bullet in your left arm that you've tried to keep quiet about," Jeff said. "So do the hay hands. The cat's out of the bag. It'll get around, no matter how many you try to buy off. A secret's no longer a secret when even two people know about it, let alone that many."

"What do you mean?" Lila cried. She had been listening, astounded.

Jeff turned toward the door to leave. She blocked his path. "Exactly what were you talking about?" she demanded.

Her father spoke. "It happens that she hasn't heard about that fellow gettin' shot in the left arm down at the Zulu camp, Temple."

"Zulu camp?" Lila's voice suddenly faltered. "You mean during—during that fight?"

"I didn't tell you the truth, dear," Mackay said. "I didn't shoot myself accidentally."

"You don't have to explain anything to me!" she burst out.

"Nobody would have believed me even if I'd told how it actually happened," Mackay said. "Not even you, darling, and you're as loyal a daughter as any man ever had. As loyal as your mother, God bless her memory."

"How did it happen?" she asked. "I'll believe you."

Jeff spoke. "Maybe you better wait awhile before making any confession, Mackay. You're in no condition—"

"It's no confession," Mackay snapped. "It's plain truth. An' I think talkin' will do me a lot of good."

"You might be right," Jeff said. "Talking is better than medicine sometimes."

"You mean that confession's good for the soul, don't you?" Mackay jeered.

He gave a grimace of pain and sank back on the pillow. Presently he was able to talk again. "I wasn't within half a mile of that Zulu camp when that poor woman was shot."

He spoke slowly as though reciting something that had happened long in the past. "I'd gone to my room at the Stockman's, but I couldn't sleep. I've paced miles of floor and miles of ground around this ranch at nights these past months since Bill Hammond an' Camo set out to smash us. I finally dressed an' sneaked out so as not to disturb Lila in the next room. I wandered around old town for a while, smokin'. I was at the graveyard when the shootin' started in the Zulu camp."

He smiled somberly at Lila. "Yeah. I was at your mother's grave. It wasn't the first time I've gone there to sit with her. Problems don't seem so big afterward."

He had to again fight off a spasm of pain. Lila took his hand.

Jeff spoke. "When Alex Crabtree gets here he'll have something that'll make the pain easier."

Mackay wagged his head impatiently. "I hurried back an' went as near the Zulu camp as I could without bein' seen. I sighted you an' Devore an' Kelso in the camp. I could hear a lot of what was said. It wasn't any place for me to be. I knew I was bein' blamed for sendin' them fools into the camp. So I went back to old town."

Lila laid a cool cloth on his forehead. His voice had been rising but he calmed again.

"I did some lookin' around on my own account," he went on. "I wandered around for quite a spell, tryin' to find out who the boys were who'd done the shootin'. Also who'd put 'em up to it."

"Are you trying to say you don't know?" Jeff demanded.

Mackay gave him a bitter, pain-twisted smile. "If I send men to fight, I ride with 'em," he said. "An' I don't put a potato sack over my head."

He saw the skepticism in Jeff's face. "To hell with you, Temple," he snarled, with a gust of fury. "I don't give a hoot whether you believe it or not. I'm only tellin' the straight of it so Lila will know what really happened."

He continued, his voice now without emotion. "I finally went back to the hotel an' got my guns. I left a note for Lila that I was goin' back to the ranch. I got my horse at the livery an' pulled out without anybody knowin'."

"You hadn't found out anything about those men?" Lila asked.

"No. I rode out to—to a certain place. I thought maybe I'd find out somethin' there."

"Tass Verity's ranch?" Jeff asked.

Mackay hesitated, then nodded. "Yes."

"To see if anyone there could get that bullet out of your arm?" Jeff demanded relentlessly.

Mackay gave him a death's-head grin. "To see if maybe Tass had anythin' to do with the shootin'. Up to that time I didn't have any bullet in my arm. Tass is mighty riled up. He's maybe got a right to be. He's a rough man. A mite too rough, maybe. I didn't hold with what had been done to the Zulus. I aimed to tell him so."

"You're doing that arm no good by all this talk," Jeff said. "You better let this wait awhile."

"I'm goin' to tell it," Mackay said grimly. "There—"

"Please, Dad!" Lila entreated. "You should rest."

". . . there was nobody at the Block T when I got there," Mackay went on. "Dark as pitch. So I went on home to the Rockin' PM. I got here before daybreak. Our place was as dark as a dungeon too. Everybody was in town. But somebody *was* here."

"Who?" Lila breathed.

"I wish I knew," Mackay said. "I put up my horse at the corral an' carried my saddle to the shed. When I stepped through the door of the shed something hit me on the head. I never saw who done it. He must have used a sandbag."

Jeff bent closer and examined Mackay's head. He ran his hand over the back of his head. There was no indication of an injury, but if a sandbag had been used, the results of any examination after so many hours would be inconclusive, no doubt.

"Go on," he said.

"It knocked me out," Mackay said. "By the time I got back to things I can remember, first daybreak had come. I had a feelin' that I'd heard riders leave. Two horses. That was about all I could remember. I tried to get to my feet. It was then that I found out I'd been shot."

Lila uttered a gasp. Her father continued in his matter-of-fact monotone. "A bullet had been shot into my left arm while I was knocked out." His head sank back exhaustedly. "So that's the story."

"And you risked losing your life or at least your arm and kept quiet about it?" Jeff asked.

"I kept quiet," Mackay said. "Just as you'd have kept quiet if you'd been in my place. Will I lose the arm?"

"You stand to lose more than that," Jeff said.

"Sure. I know. Somebody wants to hang that bloody business at the Zulu camp onto me. An' they've about done it, from the way you're lookin' at me. I knew what kind of a chance I was takin' when I tried to doctor that arm myself. I couldn't get the bullet out. My mistake was keepin' quiet about it right at the start. After that I knew nobody'd believe me."

He studied Jeff. "You don't believe me either, do you?"

"No," Jeff said.

Lila walked to where she had placed the belongings she had salvaged from the house. She found a strongbox which she opened with a key.

"We only have gold coin," she said. "No silver, unfortunately. We only deal in gold. Here's your ten dollars."

# CHAPTER ELEVEN

Jeff looked at the gold piece she placed in his hand. "And you were talking about God not long ago," he said. He tossed the coin on the floor and walked out.

The ranch house had collapsed into a burning jumble of embers whose furnace-glow lighted the surroundings. Gusts of wind stirred leaping tongues of flame from the ruins at times.

The four Mackay riders were grouped near the chuck wagon and evidently had been engaged in violent discussion. They quit talking and Jeff knew he had been the cause of dissension among them. They watched curiously as he walked past the ruins of the house and toward the east hayfield.

He paused, trying to estimate the position and the line of fire when he had traded shots with the masked rider. One of the foot-deep irrigation laterals that served the hayfield paralleled the ranch yard not far beyond the wagongate entrance to the field. The mowing machine had avoided this pitfall, leaving a thin stand of wild hay all along the course of the ditch.

This had shielded the masked man whose body lay face down in the haystubble just beyond the ditch. There was no sign of the riderless horse in the field. Jeff decided that it had found its way back through the gate and probably was on its way back to its home corral—wherever that might be.

Jeff pulled the gunnysack mask off the body. Both of his bullets had torn through the man's lungs. Life had been snuffed out instantly. Little blood had flown after he had fallen.

Jeff turned the body over. The glow of the ranch house embers was not enough for identification, nor was the moonlight, made murky by the haze of smoke. But Jeff believed he had already recognized the dead man. His hands were shaking as he searched his pocket for a match. It was his last match and he almost lost it, so uncertain were his fingers as he knelt, igniting it and shielding the flame.

He let the match gutter in the wind and die. The dead raider was Red Kramer. He knew now why Kramer had been shooting to kill. Kramer had recognized him. It had been the act of a man who feared vengeance. And whether Jeff had or had not fired instinctively and almost impersonally in self-defense would not matter now. He had slain the man who was responsible for the deaths of his parents. He knew this would be chalked up against him as an act of blood vengeance. A killing.

The Mackay crew, seeing him halted there, came walking through the gate into the hayfield, diffidently at first, and then at a run when they saw what lay in the field.

One of them said, "Good enough for the dirty nighthawkin' son."

Jeff stood staring down at Kramer's body, completely baffled. Kramer had been with Arch Stanton in the Open Switch when the Professor and Clem Devore had pointed them out as having been imported by the cattle association.

A lantern was brought. One of the Mackay riders searched Kramer's pockets. Among a thin packet of bills that Kramer carried in his pocket were two fifty-dollar banknotes. Jeff made no attempt to read the serial numbers and the Mackay men did not know that the bills meant anything to him. There was no need for close inspection. He was sure they were a part of the series of banknotes that were appearing in the hands of fighting men on both sides.

But if Kramer had been brought in by the association, why had he ridden with the Zulus against Peter Mackay's ranch? Jeff kept asking himself that question. He had no reasonable answer.

A plank was brought and Kramer's body was carried to the barn and laid out in the bed of a wagon, covered by a tarp and with a lantern suspended overhead.

A wiry Mackay man with weathered features spoke to Jeff. "How'd you know there was one of 'em down out there?"

"I saw him go down," Jeff said.

"Are you the one what got him?"

Jeff didn't answer that.

The man said, "Hank Mills an' Jim Darnell was shootin' from the bunkhouse. Maybe one of them got him."

"Maybe they did," Jeff said. "I hope so."

The man eyed Jeff for a space. "You know who he is, don't you, Temple?"

"Yes," Jeff said.

"That's more'n we do. Suppose you tell us."

"Maybe you better ask Mackay," Jeff said. "He can tell you if he wants to."

"An' why would he know the fella?"

"You better ask him that question."

Lila had joined them. She faced Jeff grimly. "Of course my father knows him. And so do I. He's Red Kramer. I told you that Kramer was working for us at the time your parents were killed."

"Maybe your father thinks he's still on the payroll," Jeff said.

"What do you mean by that?" she demanded.

Jeff looked at the ruins of the ranch house. There seemed to be no reasonable answer as to why Kramer had been with Arch Stanton by day and riding with the Zulus by night.

"I wish I knew," he admitted. "If Kramer worked for this outfit, how come these men here pretended not to recognize him?"

"I can answer that, fella," the wiry man snapped. "None of us ever saw him before. At the time Kramer worked roundup here in the hills, I was reppin' for the association up in Long Valley. These other three boys have hired up with this outfit since then. None of us knew Kramer except by reputation."

"It doesn't matter anyway," Lila said. "We had nothing to do with Kramer's personal affairs. Then or now."

She was completely sincere. That was about the only thing of which Jeff was sure. She even believed her father's story of how he had received the bullet in his arm.

Jeff looked around. His horse had been turned into the corral when he had arrived. His saddle hung on the corral poles and his camp gear was stacked beneath it.

He moved to the corral and was about to shoulder the saddle when the Mackay rider who had been doing the talking halted him and said, "Just a minute! Where you headin'?"

"Any particular reason for asking?" Jeff inquired.

"Yeah. Very particular."

"And your authority . . .?"

"I'm Steve Killian, foreman for Pete Mackay," the rider said. "If that ain't authority enough, here's—"

Killian made a move to snatch out the .45 he carried thrust in his belt. He halted, pulling in a sharp sigh, and flinching. For Jeff's hand held a six-shooter.

"You were saying . . . ?" Jeff said.

Killian was game. He was ashen, expecting to be shot, but he didn't budge. "I know your rep, Temple," he said, fighting the quiver in his voice. "You're fast. Faster'n I figured a man could be. I've got no doubt you'd shoot me. That's what Bill Hammond's payin' you to do. Go ahead. If we turn you loose now, you'd only be shootin' at us later."

Jeff knew that the other three Mackay riders had moved in to flank him. Lila came with a rush, screaming a cry of protest.

"Stop it!" she implored. "Stop it! No shooting! No shooting, for the love of heaven!"

Jeff tried to fend her off, but she swarmed on him, clamping her arms around him, forcing the gun down and driving him off balance.

"Don't!" she screamed. "Wait! Oh—!"

That was the last Jeff heard for a time. One of the riders had grasped the chance and had stepped in, swinging the barrel of his six-shooter, bringing it slashing down on his head. The scene spun wildly and he knew that he was sagging and that Lila was trying to ease his fall as he slumped down.

"You've killed him!" she was moaning.

All sounds faded.

He drifted sickly on a rough sea of semiconsciousness for a long time. At last he became sure it was Lila's face he was seeing. And that it was her hand that held him back when he tried to lift his head.

That slight effort sent him under again. Painfully he fought his way back into the light. It was lamplight. He lay in a bunk. Across from him Peter Mackay lay, watching him with feverish eyes.

Lila was saying in the querulous voice of a woman driven to exhausted desperation. "Blast it, why doesn't Doc Crabb get here?"

Jeff, with an effort of will, wagged his head slightly back and forth. The blow evidently had landed at the back of his head.

"Nothing seems busted," he croaked. He moved an arm, then the other. His legs also responded. He drew a deeper breath of satisfaction. "Minor concussion," he said. "Brought on by a blow to the supraclavicular nerves. The cervical control area was also involved, probably."

He tried to grin at Lila, even though she and the rest of the room seemed to have a tendency to float in space. "In other words, a clout on the cranium," he said. He realized that he might be babbling a little and fought to get a grip on himself.

"Don't try to talk just yet," she implored.

"How do my eyes look?" he asked.

"Well, sort of—well, does it matter?"

"Sort of crossed?" Jeff asked.

She almost wrung her hands. "Yes. But they're looking better than they were."

Things suddenly came into better focus. Jeff said, "Ah. I'm coming out of it."

"That fool Hank Mills!" Lila said. "He's young and he was excited. There was no need for hitting you."

"I don't blame Hank Mills," Jeff said. "If I remember right, it was someone else who wrapped me up for delivery. Held my arms to set me up for slugging."

"That's not true!" she cried. "Even if you deserved it."

"Is there a mirror handy that you can fetch?"

"Your eyes still won't stand still, if you must know the truth," she chattered. "They sort of keep slipping around like—like—"

"Like a pea in a shell," Jeff snarled. He was exasperated by the way his voice kept croaking. "A natural reaction. Temporary impairment of optical coordination. It's often a symptom of severe cervical concussion. Makes a man look like an idiot."

She uttered a horrified gasp. "Will it be permanent?"

Jeff's faculties were returning to something approaching normal. He grasped her arms, for she was the nearest means of support, and drew himself to a sitting position. He clung to her until the room stopped drifting and steadied. His vision began to clear.

"I believe the idiot phase is already passing," he said. "But in outward appearance only. I've got to remind myself never to let a woman set me up for a wallop on the head again."

"Quit saying that," Lila protested tearfully.

Jeff started to hoist his legs out of the bunk. He paused.

Beneath the sheet that covered him, he wore only his saddle breeches and socks. But there was a weight around his ankles. He lifted the sheet and peered.

His ankles were linked together by metal bands connected by a short length of chain. An old-style army horse hobble. The loops had been closed with baling wire, twisted firmly in place with pliers. Only pliers would open them.

Lila said, "It's for your own good. You'll be safe—here."

Jeff's gaze swung to Peter Mackay. There he met stone. Gray, unyielding stone. "You're lucky they didn't string you up to a stackin' pole, Temple," Mackay said. "You're stayin' here till this thing is settled one way or another. Whether it's for your own good or not I don't know—nor care."

"Settled?" Jeff demanded.

"You don't think us cowmen are goin' to stand still any longer an' be gobbled up piecemeal, do you? Listen!"

A persistent sound had been in the background all the time. Jeff now realized that it was the rumble of voices. A discussion was going on in the ranch yard—an angry and vehement debate.

Jeff got to his feet. He brushed Lila's hands aside when she tried to halt him, and reeled to the open door. The debris of the ranch house still cast a faint ruddy glow. The first dim pallor of dawn was in the sky.

A sizable group of men was gathered near the barn. The chuck wagon on its jacked-up wheel was being used as a rostrum. Arms were waving and voices were lifting higher in fiery debate. Many saddle horses stood in the background.

A team and a vehicle emerged from the barn. The talking ceased as they passed the group and moved out of the ranch yard, heading down the trail in the direction of Wardrum. It was Ozzie Stone, the coroner, and his death wagon, taking Red Kramer's body in charge. Jeff surmised that the inquest probably had already been held, and that he had been exonerated—officially at least.

Peter Mackay spoke, confirming this. "Nobody knows who shot Kramer. Not for sure. An' it was justifiable homicide anyway."

Jeff said nothing. Mackay spoke again. "About all of Walkin' Hills is represented out there. Tass Verity's there with half a dozen men. Evans Johnson's brought his three Rafter J boys. Sid Slater's two ridin' hands have thrown in with him an' so has most of the buckaroos from the other small outfits. Some of 'em are still driftin' in. The fire was seen a long ways, an' the word spread. Everybody guessed what had happened."

"The power and the glory of Walking Hills," Jeff said grimly.

"They're fightin' it to a finish," Mackay said. "An' I'm joinin' with 'em as soon as I kin stand square on my feet."

A dominating voice had silenced the others in the yard. "I say to burn that damned Zulu camp down, an' kick sand over the ashes. Put every lousy one of that ragtag outfit back on the Camo cars that brung 'em, an' start 'em back to where they come from."

The speaker was Tass Verity, the lanky, leathery-faced owner of Block T. He was shouting down what evidently had been a stratum of caution and opposition.

He had the backing of the big majority. Yells of approval arose. Shrill cowboy yells. Boots stamped the ground. Someone touched off a pistol in the air; the report brought a startled rumble of hoofs among the waiting horses.

"All that ain't got the guts to fight fer their own land, their own homes, their own women an' their own children, pile their saddles an' ride out o' here," Verity yelled.

He stood alone in the chuck wagon. He glared around challengingly. Not a man had the fortitude to bring down the scorn of the others by leaving.

"All right," Verity said. "We're in this together. Now, here's what—"

Someone must have warned him that Jeff was listening, for he halted abruptly and swung belligerently around to peer.

A dead silence came. Jeff moved from the doorway, forced to shuffle along in the hobbles. He was still unsteady from the blow. Lila came hurrying to help him. He pushed away the hand she placed on his arm and moved ahead. The waiting men stood stolidly eying him.

He halted. "Some of you won't come back," he said. "A lot of you. These Zulus are men just like you. They're fighting for the same things you are. Their wives, their children, homes."

"Our homes!" Tass Verity roared. "Our land. Let 'em go find their own somewhere else."

"They won't be turned away easy," Jeff said. "You'll have a battle on your hands. A tough one."

"At least there'll be one paid gun we won't have to worry

about," Verity said. "If I'd had my way we'd have strung you up, Temple. You're stayin' here."

Jeff thought of the Professor and Clem Devore. They would meet their obligations. They had taken Bill Hammond's money. They would defend the Zulus to the best of their ability. And their capabilities would be far more deadly than the ranchers realized, even though they knew the reputations of the two men.

The Professor and Clem were experienced in all the ways of protecting themselves and staying alive while they dealt the maximum damage to the opposition. They had met odds before and handled it.

Few of the ranching contingent had ever faced bullets fired in anger. None, perhaps, with the exception of Tass Verity, whose career in the Walking Hills went back to the Indian days.

"You don't know what you're walking into," Jeff said. "Go home and cool down."

He was drowned out by a fierce wave of jeering.

"Let's hit the saddle, boys!" Verity bawled. "There's too many ears around here. Too many eyes. Too many tongues to try to talk us out of what we know we've got to do if we want to stand up like men."

Verity leaped from the wagon and strode past Jeff, heading for his horse. Every man in the group followed.

There were upward of thirty of them, Jeff estimated as he watched them mount and ride away. They headed in the direction of Tass Verity's ranch, the rumble of hoofs fading.

Lila was still standing nearby. The hay hands and the cook had made themselves scarce. The Rocking PM ranch yard was deserted. Dawn was now placing a haggard gray light across the land.

Jeff hobbled to the bunkhouse. He was still unsteady on his feet, and glad to sit on one of the bunks. "Take these damned irons off me!" he said harshly.

"If you'll give your word that you won't—" she began.

"I'll give my word for nothing!" he raged. "I might be able to save the lives of some of those fools."

"Or help Ephraim Kelso and Clem Devore shoot them down," Peter Mackay said hoarsely from his bed. "The hobbles stay. There'll be a man settin' day an' night outside this bunkhouse with a buckshot gun who'll have orders to cut you in two if you try to get away."

A grizzled old saddle hand had appeared, a shotgun in his hands. He found a spot where he could be comfortable and settled down with his back against the wall of the building. From that position he commanded the door of the bunkhouse. He stood the shotgun against the wall and began tamping tobacco into his pipe.

Jeff eyed him. "Hello, Bandy! You and I rode together a couple of times on roundup."

"I'd shore be mighty sorry to have to blow a hole in you, Jeff," Bandy Peters said. "Don't make me do it."

"You're all loco!" Jeff gritted.

But he was helpless. Quicksanded. He finally hopped back to the bunk and stretched out to try to think of a way out of the situation.

Dawn had paled the glow of the lamps. Mackay had drifted off into a feverish stupor. Life for him at the moment was as uncertain and wan as the lamplight. Always it was at dawn that the fight was the hardest. Always it seemed it was then that the resolution of the human mind had reached its lowest ebb and acceptance of death was the easiest.

Lila was watching over her father. Her cheeks were thinned with weariness. Her eyes were somber and seemed bigger.

Jeff swung his hobbled legs from the bunk and moved to Peter Mackay's side. There was no way he could ease Mackay's suffering. There was little that any doctor could do that had not been done. It was up to Mackay now.

He went through the formality of testing pulse and temperature, inspecting the bandage and nodding as though satisfied. As a matter of fact, unless a turn for the better came very soon, the only hope of saving Mackay's life would be to amputate.

Lila was watching. She seemed to be reassured. This was the main reason he had carried on the performance of brisk, professional optimism. She started to frame the obvious question, but he did not want to answer it now, and forestalled it.

"Why hasn't Alex shown up?" he asked.

"The rider I sent to Wardrum was a fool," she said. "He came back from town awhile ago. He said there was nobody home at the Crabtree house. The other two doctors were off on calls too. So he left a note under the door at the Crabtree place for Doc Crabb to come out here as soon as possible."

Jeff hobbled to the door and beckoned to Bandy. He indicated that he wanted to speak out of range of Lila's ears.

The old man shuffled warily nearer, the hammer of the shotgun under his thumb. "No capers now, Jeff," he warned.

"Send another rider to town," Jeff whispered. "Fast! Go yourself, if there's nobody else. Try to find Alex Crabtree. If he isn't around, get one of the other doctors. And if they're not to be found, get hold of Aunt Hettie Crabtree. Tell her I need tools for an amputation. She'll know what to send."

"So the boss is goin' to lose his arm, huh?" Bandy said morosely. "Shame. Anyway, it's his left. He kin still rope an' cuss." He gave Jeff a lowering scowl. "I know you think he killed them Zulus. I heard about them killin's. If the boss said he shot hisself accidental, then that's what he done. He ain't a man to lie."

Bandy added, "I'll send that young Ronnie Smith from the hayin' crew. He's anxious to git to town anyway. Got a girl there."

Bandy went hurrying to the barn where the hay hands, displaced from the bunkhouse by Mackay's ordeal, were sleeping.

"Ronnie!" Bandy bawled. "Roust out! Shake a laig! You're goin' to town. I'll ketch you up a horse. That flashy roan from the boss's string thet you've been wantin' to ride."

Jeff hopped to the corral and halted the lanky young hay hand as he was about to mount the horse that Bandy had roped and saddled. "Listen to me, and listen close, Ronnie," he said. "I want no more mistakes. Either fetch a doctor back with you or bring the tools I'll need. Understand?"

Ronnie nodded, his Adam's apple bobbing. "One more thing," Jeff said. "If anybody asks you what this is all about, just tell them one of the hay hands fell under the mower and got hurt."

He watched the messenger ride away, tense with pride at being allowed to ride the roan.

Peter Mackay knew nothing of all this. He still lay in a daze, breathing laboriously. Jeff again counted pulse and tested temperature.

"He's at least losing no ground," he told Lila.

He peered closer at her. "There'll be another patient to worry about if you don't get some rest. You need a bath to settle your nerves and some solid sleep."

He hopped to the door. The cook had started his morning chores, for smoke was rising from the chimney of his shack.

Bandy was on guard outside the door. "Tell the cook to get warm water and a tub ready," Jeff said. "Fetch it into the bunkhouse, along with towels."

He spoke to Lila. "We'll send you some breakfast when you're ready. When I come back from eating I want to find you asleep."

She said meekly, "Yes." She gave him a slanting look and added, "Yes, Doctor."

Jeff gave her a glare. His head still throbbed from the blow he had taken. His eyes were red from loss of sleep. His temper was rubbed raw.

"How about these hobbles?" he snarled at Bandy. "And put that infernal gun away before I wrap it around your ugly neck. I'm too tired to run, even if I was of a mind."

Bandy backed off a step or two, looking anxiously to Lila for advice. She nodded and said, "Take off the hobbles."

Bandy didn't like the idea, but he finally laid the shotgun aside, produced a pair of pliers and freed the wires on the loops. He seized up the hobbles and scuttled out of reach.

"I'll be watchin' you, Jeff," he warned. "I'll put them irons back on you unless you toe chalk."

Jeff strode angrily to the cookhouse. Bandy followed him, the shotgun ready, the hobbles dangling from his belt. Under the lash of Jeff's tongue, the Chinese cook began moving at full speed. Bandy and the cook soon hurried off to the bunkhouse, lugging a wooden tub of bath water.

Jeff ate a solid breakfast of steak, flapjacks, scrambled eggs and canned fruit that the cook heaped on the table for the benefit of the haying crew and Bandy as well as himself.

He felt more amiable toward the world when he rolled a cigaret. The bunkhouse was silent when he approached it. He moved to the door and peered in.

Lila was asleep in one of the bunks, only her tawny hair visible back of a quilt she had draped from the upper frame.

Her father's eyes were closed also. Jeff tiptoed to his side. Mackay was in real sleep now, rather than the stupor of fever. A turn for the better had come.

Jeff left the bunkhouse. Followed by the faithful Bandy

and the shotgun, he got his bedroll and walked to the barn. There he spread his tarp and quilts on a pile of hay. Within seconds he was asleep.

# CHAPTER TWELVE

It was nearly noon when he awakened completely. Bandy, who had been dozing nearby, aroused and reached for his shotgun.

"Bandy," Jeff said. "I could have possumed sleep and injuned up on you half a dozen times, if I'd wanted to. Why don't you get rid of that thing before you blow off a toe?"

"I'd lose more'n a toe if you got away from here," Bandy said mournfully. "You ain't never seen Lila when she got riled. I'd as soon tangle with a herd of wolverines."

Jeff doused his head in a basin at the wash bench. He walked to the bunkhouse, running his hand over jaws that were in need of a shave.

Lila and her father were still asleep. He entered quietly. Mackay was definitely much improved. His temperature was still up, but it was no longer a devastating fire.

Jeff stood looking down at his patient. In Jeff was a knowledge of achievement. Of triumph. Also a peace of mind he had not known in more than three years—not since the terrible moment when Angelina Simmons had died on his operating table.

He discovered that Lila had awakened and was watching him. "Dad's better, isn't he?" she whispered. "I can see it in your face."

Jeff nodded. "He's better." He added, "At the moment at least."

He did not want to arouse too much hope in her. It was too early to be sure, but he was beginning to believe that the instruments he had sent for would not be needed. Peter Mackay's arm might be saved.

But soon the doubts came flooding back. And the shadows. The shadowing memory of Angie dying in his desperate hands. Of his mother whom Alex had been unable to save. Of Clem Devore's invalid wife. Of all the failures, all the despairs, all the heartaches.

Lila had dressed. She came to his side. "What is it?" she asked. "What happened? You look so—so lost!"

A step sounded at the door. The Professor spoke in his precise diction. "The lion is the prisoner of the dove, I see."

The Professor stood in the open door of the bunkhouse. He was freshly-shaven, apple-ruddy, his eyes twinkling. His tall hat was dusty from a journey, but it was tilted at a jaunty angle. He had found a wildflower blooming and had fixed it in the buttonhole of his frock coat, whose creases also bore dust of the trail.

At his shoulder Clem Devore was grinning. Clem clasped the arm of Bandy Peters, who bore a sheepish expression. Clem was in possession of Bandy's buckshot gun.

Peter Mackay awakened. He lifted his head, gazing at the Professor and Clem. "Now we've got all three of you to buck," he said to Jeff.

The Professor removed his hat in deference to Lila. "We decided to take a drive through the country," he explained to Jeff. "There were rumors in Wardrum last night that a big fire had been sighted in the direction of the Mackay ranch. Knowing that you have a bad habit of getting yourself involved in other persons' misfortunes, we came this way."

"To get involved also?" Jeff inquired.

The Professor waved that aside. "We found this old reprobate asleep on his feet just outside the door," he said. "When we accosted him, his attitude was very hostile. We took him into custody and looked farther. And our quest ended here. Lo, we find you standing like a conqueror over a vanquished foe, with a beautiful damsel lurking in the offing. This surly individual who lies there glaring at us is Peter Mackay, owner of this ranch, of course?"

Lila answered grimly. "He is."

"And the injury from which he is suffering?" the Professor inquired politely. "Bitten by a grizzly, perhaps?"

"In the left arm," Clem said. "One of these here Winchester grizzlys."

"I know what you're trying to say," Lila said. "You're wrong."

The iron hobbles still dangled on Bandy's belt. Jeff seized them, walked to the door and hurled them far across the ranch yard.

"Temper! Temper!" the Professor said chidingly. "I would say that you're a man at the end of his patience."

"How did you two get here?" Jeff asked. "Saddleback?"

"I've reached an age and weight wherein I prefer more comfort," the Professor said. "We rented a rig at the livery. We left it in the brush a short distance out. We had discovered that the house had been burned. We suspected our presence might not be welcome. Therefore the precautions."

"A bunch of men shot up this place last night and touched off the house," Jeff said.

"Hell's to pay and they're heating the pitch," Clem observed.

"An eye for an eye," the Professor said. "A tooth for a tooth. The Zulus, of course. They paid off for the raid on their camp."

"There's going to be more than eyes clawed out," Jeff said. "The ranchers are on the prod. An army of them rode away from here about daylight, with Tass Verity acting as general. They aim to burn the Zulu camp and run every one of them out of the country."

"We didn't see any sign of any army heading for Wardrum," Clem said.

"They'd hardly make any kind of a move in daylight," Jeff said. "They're probably holed up at Verity's place, waiting until dark. They seemed to be heading in that direction when they pulled out of here."

"In that case there's no great rush in returning to Wardrum," the Professor said. "We have time to take on a little food and rest." He added, hopefully, "And perhaps a mild libation if one is available."

"If not, there's a bottle under the seat of the buggy," Clem said. "I saw you cache it there when we set out this morning, Ephraim."

The Professor was not embarrassed. "I merely prepared for drought, Clement."

"Let it stay there," Jeff said. "We're still on the Injun list, remember. Gunpowder and firewater don't mix."

"As you wish," the Professor said sadly.

Jeff motioned them outside and they walked away from the bunkhouse to talk. He repeated Peter Mackay's story of how he had been shot.

The Professor thoughtfully removed his hat, dusted it and smoothed the nap on his sleeve. "The only item in Mackay's favor, I would say, is that his story is so fantastic I wonder if he could have conceived it. A person who invents a lie usually concocts some tale that is at least plausible."

"What's happening in Wardrum?" Jeff asked.

"Old town's closed up tight as a coffin," Clem said. "When word was whispered around of the fire at the Mackay place, they buttoned up to the chin and locked on the storm shutters. A man can't even buy sody pop."

"It's much different in new town," the Professor said. "Hammond Street is wide open and steaming. The Zulus seem to have come into some spending money. They are using it to buy courage. Whisky courage."

"Camo money, of course," Clem said.

"What about Alex Crabtree?" Jeff asked. "Word was left for him to come out here and take care of Mackay, but he's never shown up. I sent another boy a couple of hours ago to fetch him."

"That must have been the lad we passed on the trail," the professor said. "He should be in Wardrum by this time. Dr. Alex was still sleeping when we pulled out this morning. We made a very early start."

"What about this fight here last night?" Clem asked. "Where were you when the Zulus hit?"

Jeff was silent for a moment. "I took a hand in it," he said.

They eyed him. "With the Zulus?" Clem asked.

"No. One of them singled me out and tried to put a slug in me. I drew on him."

They waited. Their casual manner had vanished. Steel had edged to the surface.

"Red Kramer," Jeff said. "He's dead."

"But—" Clem began.

"I know," Jeff said. "He was one of Arch Stanton's bunch. And Stanton's supposed to be working for the ranchers."

"Kramer's the kind who'd back-stab his own brother if there was a dollar in it," Clem said uneasily. "He's probably takin' money from both sides."

"The same kind of money?" Jeff asked. "He was carrying a couple of those crisp new fifties. They're beginning to look familiar."

They stood in lowering silence. Jeff spoke. "I'm wondering how many more are carrying money from both sides."

"Apparently a very large double cross is being perpetrated," the Professor said.

"On somebody," Clem said.

"That somebody might be us," Jeff said.

He stood running his hand over his unshaven chin. "And here's something else I've been puzzling over. If Arch Stanton and his crew have been hired by the cattlemen, where were they last night when Tass Verity was organizing his army? From what I saw, every man was a genuine Walking Hills cowhand or owner. In fact, I knew the most of them. They used to be friends of mine. They're men who've been around here for years."

"And now you have no friends in the Walking Hills," the Professor said.

They were silent for a time. "Arch Stanton was in Wardrum last night," Clem said. "I saw him in the Open Switch. That was just about the time the Professor and me headed back to the Crabtree house to turn in. About eleven o'clock. We had been in town since after supper, but hadn't been in the Open Switch all the time. We hit a few other places."

"Who was with him?"

"Nobody. He was alone."

"I spotted riders heading down the country yesterday afternoon as I rode along the trail toward the Little Beaver," Jeff said. "They were keeping below the skyline as much as they could. I'm sure one was Bass Brackett. I couldn't make out anything about the others."

"If Brackett was there, then it's easy to guess who the rest of 'em were," Clem observed. "Fletch Jones, Red Kramer and these other hard cases who've been hanging around with Arch."

"I had the impression they were heading for Tass Verity's Block T," Jeff said.

"I see your point, Jefferson," the Professor said. "If they were in this neck of the woods, why weren't they hurrying to protect this ranch when the house was burning? Where were they when Verity was here, organizing the cattlemen?"

"Exactly," Jeff said.

"The longer we pound this thing," Clem said, "the more it gives off the sound of a cracked bell."

"Real, genuine phony," Jeff said.

"It could be that we're being used as pigeons to lure the real quarry within reach," the Professor commented.

"Pigeons generally get caught in the cross-fire," Clem said. "An' that's no place to be, as my grandpap told me when I was ankle high to a short cricket."

"I'm wondering if maybe the cattlemen are the ones who are going to find themselves right in the middle along with us," Jeff observed.

"If so, they have it coming," the Professor said sourly. "The methods of the cattlemen have not earned my respect, to say the least. They are murderers. They are an abomination unto the Lord."

Lila stepped out of the door of the nearby wagonshed. "That's a terrible thing to say!" she cried. She was angry, so angry her lips were pale. "Yes!" she said. "I've been eavesdropping."

She glared at the Professor. "I never heard such an unfair thing in my life. Nor such a brutal thing."

Clem spoke. "We don't hold with killin' women." His own face was bleak, unrelenting.

"My father had nothing to do with that Zulu woman's death," she said.

She watched their faces and seemed to find only disbelief. She caught Clem by the arms, trying to shake him. "It's the truth! You're blind! All of you! Does Dad look like a man who'd kill a woman? Or a man? Why, he even told me he had taken a liking to Ralph Slocum."

She found Clem unyielding. She released him. She was fighting back tears. "Get off this ranch," she said slowly, choosing her words. "All three of you. When you believe a lie, you're liars. Whether you take Camo money or not doesn't matter. You're against us. That's all that matters."

"We're against women-killers," Clem said harshly.

She turned and almost ran from them and into the bunkhouse. Jeff stood watching her. He was thinking that there might never be another meeting between them.

"I'll catch up my horse," he said. "We better be heading for Wardrum."

The Professor spoke. "Aren't you overlooking something, Jefferson? If I understood her correctly she said that her father had taken a liking to Ralph Slocum."

Jeff halted in stride. He looked wildly at the Professor. "Of course!"

Then he went moving in long strides to the bunkhouse. Lila backed away when he entered and stood close by her father's bunk.

"What was that you just said?" Jeff demanded.

"I meant every word of it," she said.

"I mean that part about your father having taken a liking to Ralph Slocum."

"I don't understand," she said.

Peter Mackay was awake and staring. His eyes were rational.

"Did you know Ralph Slocum personally, Mackay?" Jeff asked.

"Know him?" Mackay was puzzled by the question. "I'd hardly say that. I only talked to him once."

"But you *had* talked to him?"

Mackay's mind was still not quite up to this. Lila answered for him. "Mr. Slocum met Dad in Wardrum on the street."

"How long ago?"

"Why—why, it was on Saturday. Saturday, a week ago."

"What did they talk about?"

"Mr. Slocum asked if there wasn't some way the opening of the Hills could be worked out without hurting anyone."

Mackay spoke. "He seemed to be an honest sort of man. I respected him, even if he was a Zulu. We might have figured out somethin', except that Tass showed up. Then the beans were spilled for fair."

"How was that?"

"Tass hates Zulus. Him an' Slocum come mighty near fightin' it out right there in the street. I held 'em apart. Slocum still had his hackles up when he walked away. I raked Tass over the coals for it. He's a hard man. I got to admit that. He's mighty bullheaded."

The Professor and Clem were listening. Clem shrugged skeptically. The Professor merely shrugged.

The three of them moved outside to talk. "Perhaps we've been baying the wrong tree after all," the Professor said. "Perhaps the possum's elsewhere."

"Maybe it was this Tass Verity," Clem said.

Jeff shook his head. "We're up against the same dead end there. Mackay just told us that Slocum and Tass Verity had almost come to blows not long ago. Slocum wouldn't forget a man like that. He said he could identify the man who killed the Barnes woman if he ever laid eyes on him again. I took it that he didn't think he'd ever seen the man before."

"But the fellow had a sack or some such mask over his head," the Professor said. "And wore a slicker. Slocum couldn't have seen his face."

"Of course," Clem exclaimed. "We're wasting time. This thing of Slocum and Mackay having met before doesn't mean a thing. He must have noticed something about the killer that would identify him later."

Jeff drew a long sigh. "I'm afraid you're right. Slocum mentioned that he'd know the killer the same way Jennie Barnes had identified him."

"*Afraid* we're right?" Clem challenged grimly. "You were hoping it wouldn't be Mackay, weren't you?"

"Yes," Jeff said reluctantly.

Clem softened. "I'm sorry. But he's our man. After all, he's the one with the slug in his arm. And he had tried to keep it quiet."

"It's possible there *might* be another man with a wounded arm," the Professor said.

"Do we go around asking every jasper we meet to roll up his left sleeve so we can take a look?" Clem asked.

"That is not up to us, Clement," the Professor said. "That is the responsibility of the law."

"Law?" Clem laughed jeeringly. "You don't think Lish Carter's goin' to get himself in a sweat tryin' to find out which cattlemen it was that raided the Zulus. He's a cowman himself. Cattlemen elected him sheriff. An' the town marshal's stayin' clear. No jurisdiction. The Zulu camp is outside the town limits. The law in these parts is cattlemen's law."

"I fear you are correct," the Professor said. "We will have no help from the law if we attempt to see that the Zulus get justice. And no sympathy."

He turned, lifting his head, sniffing. The aroma of food drifted from the cookhouse. The haying crew was heading back from the fields for dinner.

"I'd give a pretty penny for a morsel of food at this moment," he said mournfully. "But, since we are not welcome . . ."

He had lifted his voice deliberately, so that it reached Lila, who had been standing in the door of the bunkhouse, eying them.

"I'll tell the cook to feed you," she said abruptly.

"Then we are no longer unwelcome?" the Professor exclaimed, beaming.

She addressed Jeff. "I was being ungrateful. I appreciate what you did for us—for my father."

"To forgive is divine, fair lady," the Professor said. "To feed the hungry is angelic."

"It's only fair to tell you that I'm going to ride over to

Block T and warn Mr. Verity and the others," she said. "I'm going to tell them that Jeff Temple is loose and that you two are here also and that they're not only going to be up against the Zulus but—but—"

She hesitated. Jeff tersely supplied the words. "Professional gunfighters."

"Yes," she said.

"If it'll make you feel any better, go ahead," Jeff said. "But it'll be a waste of time. It's a cinch they spotted Clem and the Professor on their way here. Quite a stretch of the trail is in sight from Block T."

She thought it over. "You're probably right," she admitted. "But I want to make sure they know."

The cook began swinging the brass dinner bell.

"What should I give father to eat?" she asked.

"Solid grub," Jeff said. "There's nothing wrong with his teeth. He's a man used to square meals. He needs them now."

"He's going to be all right, isn't he?" she asked. "Even—even his arm."

"It's his neck now that he'll have to worry about," Jeff said.

She seemed to sag a little. "I had started to think you were believing that he had told the truth."

She turned and walked tiredly to the cookhouse. The hay hands were already lined up at the log table in the eating room. Jeff followed her into the kitchen and watched as she prepared a tray of food for her father.

He spoke abruptly. "Why do you tag Tass Verity as *Mister* Verity?"

She paused, a ladle in her hand. "Do I?"

"Folks who are neighbors—and allies—usually aren't that formal," Jeff said. "At least not the way you use that handle."

"And how do I use it?"

"Sort of like it was a pitchfork to keep *Mister* Verity at a distance where he won't contaminate you. Or maybe sort of like you wish you were sticking that pitchfork into his hide."

"I hadn't noticed that I use a pitchfork."

"Let's say it's a way you have of rating him in your tally book."

"You mean among the culls?"

Jeff grinned. "I'd say you peg him just a little lower than a knob-kneed, twisthorn leppie in heelfly time."

"I suppose you're entitled to any interpretation you want to put on my pitchfork tongue," she said. "We're in this with Mister Verity. We hang and rattle together."

Jeff tried another tack. "If cattlemen push this thing to a gunfight, they'll lose, even if they win the fight. They might scare the Zulus out, but a lot of the ranchers won't be alive to celebrate. But more than that, it'll lash back on them. Teddy Roosevelt's the kind of a man who'll get redheaded and sign the Camo charter, just to cut the cattlemen down to size."

"You may be right," she admitted.

"Tass Verity seems to be the one doing the pushing. But many a man has bogged his herd in a mudhole because he was too obstinate to take advice."

"It must run in the family," she said. "Bill Hammond won't give an inch either."

"In the family?"

"Bill Hammond is Tass Verity's nephew," she said. "His mother was a Verity. I took it for granted you knew that."

"I didn't know it," Jeff said.

She left then, carrying the tray. He joined the men at the table. The cook began hurrying in with bowls and platters of food.

# CHAPTER THIRTEEN

Jeff ate thoughtfully. The blood relationship of Bill Hammond and Tass Verity could explain Verity's visit to Hammond's office the night Jeff had seen him there. They could still adhere to family ties, even though on opposite sides of the fence in financial matters. But, knowing the two men, Jeff doubted that in their cases blood would be thicker than a bankroll. And, above all, there was the air of evasiveness, furtiveness.

He sat, nursing his coffee mug, long after the others had finished. The hay hands were on their way back to the field. Clem and the Professor had moved outside to smoke.

Lila returned, bringing the tray of empty dishes. "Dad *is* better," she said happily. "He was really hungry."

The cook came hurrying to serve her with food he had

kept warm. Jeff sat across the table from her with his coffee.

"Alex Crabtree said your father had a hard pull in building up his Angus herd," he said.

"Yes," she said. "But he was seeing his way clear when this Zulu trouble started."

"How clear?"

"He'd got out of debt as far as the land is concerned, but the cattle are still mortgaged."

"Who loaned the money? The Wardrum Stockman's National?"

"Yes. But the bank sold the mortgage later on."

"To Tass Verity?"

She nodded. "There's nothing wrong with that, is there?"

"It's regular procedure. Tass has made about as much money that way as out of cattle. The bank charged your father a commission for making the loan. Tass bought the paper at a discount. Cattle are a risk, of course. You usually have to pay around ten per cent interest."

"Compounded quarterly," she said.

"Is that why you call him *Mister* Verity?"

"Not exactly. But what should I call him?"

"A number of things, I imagine, if you weren't a lady."

She smiled. "Even so, Dad says that in a year or so we'll have the cattle clear of debt. We've really no complaint against Tass Verity. He's only doing what everyone else does who loans money on cattle."

Jeff sat rubbing his chin, thinking. "None of this tallies up," he said. "Tass is a dollar-squeezer. I rode beef roundup for him a couple of times. He always saw to it that you earned your pay, but he fed well and you rode good horseflesh. Naturally, he'd jump at the chance to take over a paying proposition like this outfit, but if he and Hammond are in cahoots, it seems to me they're going about it in an expensive way."

"We've had the same thought," she said. "Dad has built up a herd, but it's only a foundation. It will grow into something big with hard work and good luck, but that would take years. After all, nine hundred head of Angus isn't exactly a fortune. In addition, if the settlers move in, *Mister* Verity's Block T will be hit hard too."

She smiled wryly as she put the emphasis on the title.

"He won't be wiped clear out, like you people probably will," Jeff said. "He can still run cattle in that rough country beyond the bluffs. The Zulus won't bother him there.

Even so, he'll be hurt. It looks like a losing proposition for him no matter how you size it up."

He heard Clem calling him, and walked outside. Clem had climbed a ladder-stair into a cottonwood tree near the bunkhouse. A platform had been built high in the branches, and the binoculars that Lila had mentioned were mounted there. Clem had removed the canvas cover and was peering through the glasses.

"I'm lookin' right smack dab into Verity's ranch yard," he said.

"And what do you see?" the Professor demanded impatiently.

"Nothin'."

"Bah!" the Professor snorted.

"There's nobody in sight," Clem said. "Nothin' movin'. Not even a jaybird hoppin' around. Corral's empty too. But the crowd's still there somewhere."

"How do you know?" Jeff asked.

"I see the shine of dust from beyond the house," Clem explained. "Looks like they've got their horses staked out of sight below some cutbanks just beyond the spread."

Jeff climbed the ladder to the platform and gazed through the glasses. "They're holed up in the house," he decided. "They're sitting tight until dark."

He scanned the landscape in the direction of Wardrum, but there was nothing moving, on the trail at least. He spent time inspecting the Walking Hills in all directions as far as the glasses reached. The only living things that he found were range cattle, both Mackay black Angus and whiteface stock from other outfits.

He swung the glasses southward. The lens picked up the stakes marking the right-of-way that Camo had surveyed in that direction. The glasses were powerful. The bulk of the Grindstones came into focus, a weather-wrinkled gray wall, desolate and forbidding.

Jeff had hunted mountain lion and bighorns in the canyons of the Grindstones and had found them to be a test of endurance for both himself and his horses.

"How's Camo going to get through the Grindstones?" he called down to Lila.

She came lithely up the ladder and huddled on the platform at his side. "Through Granite Canyon, they say," she said. "But the cowboys say that part of it hasn't been surveyed. Camo's been waiting to get its charter before spending any more money."

Jeff was about to end his peering, when he halted the glasses, shortened the focus and studied a small, cleared area along the Camo right-of-way. Lifting his head and gazing with the unaided eye, he saw that it was scarcely a mile away and not far beyond a flat where the Rocking PM had built its dipping tanks and squeezer chutes for use at branding time.

He motioned Lila to take over the glasses. "That's the place where Camo drilled," she said. "It's just off our property line."

"Drilled? For what?"

"Water. What else?"

"Did they find any?"

"Mister Verity says they didn't. He felt happy about it."

"Happy?"

"Well, 'vindicated' would be a better word for it. He had drilled for water all over the Hills more than two years ago. It cost him a pretty penny, even though he did the drilling himself. He had experience at drilling in his younger days. He bought a secondhand drilling rig, but he had to hire men to help him run it."

"And he never found any water?"

"No. He was sure there was an underground river under his ranch and ours that would turn the Hills into a paradise. But if it's there he didn't find it."

"You say this was two years ago?"

"Let me think. Yes, it was all of that. He drilled most of the summer. He drilled on our place too. Four or five holes on a line from east to west. One spot was out there back of the wagonshed."

"You're not saying that he drilled on Mackay land at his own expense?"

"Yes. He'd got stubborn about it. He'd taken a lot of joshing about this underground river. Some people even thought he was a little touched in the head."

"Spending money on another man's land doesn't exactly sound like Tass was in his right mind," Jeff said.

She shrugged. "He asked permission from Dad. There couldn't be any harm in it. And if he had hit water we'd have been riding high."

"Oil!" Clem exclaimed. "That's it. There's oil here."

Lila smiled wryly. "We thought of that. But there's no oil in the Walking Hills. Geologists say it's impossible. It has something to do with the rock formation."

"There's no water either, except in Little Beaver," Jeff said. "Lots of holes were punched years ago all over the Hills. That dream about an underground river comes from way back. And that's what it is. A dream. Tass knows that. Bill Hammond must know it too. But you say Camo drilled on that spot down there. How long ago?"

"Last fall. Mister Verity sold them his drill rig. It was about the only money he got back."

Jeff looked at Clem. "Why would they want to drill for water there anyway?" he asked. "That's only a mile or so from Little Beaver. If they wanted a watering tank out here, it'd be easier and cheaper to pump it out of the stream. And in the second place why would they need water this close to Wardrum?"

"How deep did they drill, Miss Lila?" Clem asked.

"I have no idea. I don't think anyone knows. The drilling crew wouldn't talk. And when they quit they vanished overnight. Nobody could even find the exact spot where they drilled. The boys say a scraper was run over the place before they pulled out. The only thing I ever found out there, was a short piece of round rock that looked like they must have drilled it out. I came across it in the sagebrush one day when I was looking around out there."

"Round rock?" Jeff questioned.

"Well, not like a ball. Like a cylinder."

"Core," Jeff said. "They had core-drilled. That's how they sample the rock structure. But they wouldn't be likely to go to the trouble of core-drilling if they were after water. Is this core that you found still around?"

She clasped both hands to her cheeks, trying to rack her memory. "I haven't seen it for a long time. I had almost forgotten about it. It didn't seem important. Maybe it's in the ashes of the house."

"What did it look like?"

"Why—why, nothing unusual. Sort of a faded blue. It did have some green specks."

Bandy Peters, who had been listening from the ground, spoke. "Tass Verity took thet chunk o' rock, Lila."

They peered down. "Verity?" Jeff asked. "Why would he have taken it?"

"Dunno," Bandy said. "Tass always was sort of a pack rat. Saves string, old nails. Guess he figured it'd come in handy sometime. He took it quite awhile ago. It'd been layin' around the yard. I happen to remember it, for I got a snicker out of the way old Tass sneaked it under his jacket an' hit the saddle for home. He thought nobody had seen him. It wasn't worth stealin', but he stole it."

Jeff discovered that a streamer of dust had appeared on the swells north of the stream. He swung the glasses in that direction.

"It's that young hay hand we sent to town," he said. "Ronnie Smith. He's in a hurry. He's got himself a fresh horse in Wardrum so as to make fast tracks."

They descended into the yard to meet the youth who rode in. Dust and lather coated the animal and spattered the horseman.

Ronnie singled out Jeff and began talking even before he swung stiffly down. "Mis' Crabtree wants you to come to Wardrum, Mr. Temple!" he croaked from a dry throat. "Right away!"

"Aunt Hettie Crabtree? What's happened?"

"She said she's worried nigh to death about Doctor Crabtree. She's afeared somethin's happened to him."

"You mean he's missing?"

"He went away on a call last night an' ain't never come back. That's all I know."

Jeff whirled on the Professor and Clem. "You said—" he began.

"We understood that the doctor was asleep in his room when we left," the Professor said. "As we told you, we left town early this morning. Miss Hettie got breakfast for us. She asked us to be quiet so as not to disturb him."

Clem nodded. "She said he must have been up until all hours with a patient an' that he hadn't been sleepin' too well anyway lately because of worryin' about all this Zulu trouble. She wanted him to get some rest."

Jeff headed for the corral. "Bandy! Fetch a catch rope! I want the top horse in the string."

"An' one for me too," Clem said as he joined in the rush. "An' a saddle."

They were mounted within minutes. Peter Mackay had left his bunk and was in the door, watching. "Get back in bed!" Jeff roared at him. "Do you want to start that arm going again?"

But Mackay remained there as he and Clem rode out of the yard. Lila stood alone in the sunshine. She had lifted an arm, as though to stop them, then had let it fall to her side. The Professor was waddling away to find the livery rig in which he and Clem had arrived.

Looking back, Jeff saw Lila climbing the ladder to the platform in the cottonwood. Presently he could make out only the green canopy of the tree above the swells, but he knew that she was still there, watching through the binoculars.

Soon this was lost too. They rode through the undulating gray-green sea of the Walking Hills toward Wardrum, with nothing ahead or astern except the plume of dust from the buggy in which the Professor was following them at a fast pace.

## CHAPTER FOURTEEN

The sun had set and the long twilight was beginning to lose out to the coming night when they alighted from their jaded horses at the Crabtree house.

Hettie was already hurrying from the house to meet them. "Alex—?" Jeff began, but he could see the answer in her face.

Hettie burst into tears. "No word!" she sobbed. "Not a thing. He never stayed away even a few hours without lettin' me know where he was."

Jeff led her into the house, with Clem following. The Professor arrived in the buggy and joined them.

"Tell us about it," Jeff said. "Where did Alex go?"

"I don't know," she said wearily. "I went to prayer meeting last night at the church. It was about nine o'clock when I got home. Alex wasn't here, but I didn't think anything of it. He often walks uptown to buy a glass of beer and play checkers at Ed Lowery's place. I always know where to find him. If he goes on a call he always writes on a blackboard in his office where he'll be."

Jeff looked at Clem and the Professor. "This was while you two were uptown?"

Hettie answered. "Yes. None of them had got home by the time I went to bed. Mr. Kelso and Mr. Devore got up early. They said they were going on quite a trip. I cooked them some breakfast. I listened at Alex's door, but didn't hear anything, so I decided he was still asleep. I could see by the looks of his office that he'd had a patient durin' the night. Strange they didn't wake me up. It wasn't till a couple of hours later that I began to get worried an' looked in at Alex's room. He wasn't there. He hadn't been there all night. His bed hadn't been slept in."

Jeff walked into Alex's medical shop. It was in spic-and-span order with every item of equipment in its proper place.

He looked at the blackboard on which Alex chalked any messages he wanted to leave for Hettie. The last scribbled item had been partly erased, and evidently was days old.

"He never fails to leave word when he goes away," Hettie wailed. "I expected to find a message when I scrubbed up an' straightened up the place. That's when I first started to get worried."

"Scrubbed up?" Jeff questioned. "You said he must have had a patient here in his office during the night."

"Yes. Things were in an awful mess."

"What things?"

"Why—why, his operatin' instruments."

"What instruments?"

"Why, the scalpel had been used. And the clamps. The probe too. He'd done some stitchin'. An' bandagin'. Somebody must have got hurt. Alex had tried to straighten things up, but he must have left before he got finished."

"You said you didn't hear anything during the night?" Jeff asked.

"Not a thing. An' I'm a light sleeper."

"Do you generally wake up when Alex gets a night call?"

"Always. They always pound on the door enough to wake the dead."

"Did you look into this shop when you came home from church?"

"Why—why no. Not till this mornin'."

"Then whoever this patient was might have come here while you were at church," Jeff said. "Early in the evening. You don't know for sure that Alex even had a late call."

He walked to the cabinet close by the operating table in which Alex kept his surgical instruments and other supplies. It contained upward of a score of drawers of all shapes and sizes.

Jeff was familiar with this cabinet, which had served Alex for years. He was familiar also with Alex's habits, for he had spent as much time as possible in this room whenever he was home during his medical training.

He opened a small drawer. It contained a collection of oddly-assorted objects. Safety pins and buttons of many sizes. Birdshot and buckshot. Broken blades of penknives and even of a Bowie knife. A dozen or more bullets of various calibers, along with other nondescript objects.

These were souvenirs of a doctor's profession that had been extracted from the flesh or the stomachs of patients. Alex had a habit of dropping these items in the cabinet drawer in order to use them as case examples for the extemporaneous lectures he liked to deliver for the benefit of anyone who might be interested.

Jeff examined the slugs. The majority were damaged and some were flattened out of all semblance of their original shapes. Nearly all had been in the drawer for some time, for they had taken on the dull patina of disuse.

However, one seemed to be a new addition. It was only slightly flattened, and the marks of the instrument that had been used to extract it were still bright in the metal.

Jeff handed it to the Professor, who examined it and passed it to Clem.

"A .44-40," Clem said, tossing it back to Jeff.

The Professor said casually, "I recall that Ralph Slocum's rifle was one of those old .44s. It was my favorite weapon in its day."

"Maybe its day isn't over with yet," Jeff said.

He pocketed the bullet. He prowled the shop, but found nothing more that might offer information. He walked through the kitchen to the stableyard at the rear. Clem and the Professor and Hettie followed him.

He rolled open the sliding door of the stable in which Alex quartered his horses and vehicle. Alex always maintained three top-quality carriage animals in addition to the saddle horse he had loaned Jeff. "One for speed, one for mud and one for looks," was his way of explaining this extravagance.

Alex's buggy stood in its usual place on the carriageway. The three harness animals were in their box stalls, stamping and hungry, for their mangers were empty and so were their water tubs.

"Why, I—I took it for granted that Alex had taken the rig when he went away," Hettie stammered.

"It looks like nobody's been here since yesterday," Jeff said. "The horses haven't been fed."

"I never looked in the stable today," Hettie quavered. "I'm afeared of horses. When Alex expects to be gone overlong he generally gives them enough hay and water to carry them an' lets them have the run of the stableyard. Either that or he asks Sam Eilers at the livery to come down and take care of them."

The three men prowled the interior of the stable. It was Jeff who found Alex Crabtree.

Alex's body was huddled back of a box of galvanized iron in which corn and bran were stored. He was partly covered by straw that had been forked over him. His legs were in sight.

"Take Aunt Hettie out of here," Jeff said.

Hettie had glimpsed her brother's body. She buried her face in her hands and began to weep. The Professor placed an arm around her and led her to the house.

Clem brought a lap robe from the buggy and spread it on the floor. He and Jeff lifted Alex's body from its hiding place.

Jeff suddenly bent closer. He placed an ear to Alex's chest. He pushed back an eyelid, peering in the dim light. "He's alive!" he exclaimed.

He added, "But not by much!"

Alex's pulse was the merest uncertain flutter. Jeff could find no sign of respiration at all. He placed his mouth to Alex's and forced breath into the lungs. Alex's pulse did not respond.

Jeff fought panic. "Bring lamps!" he said. "I need light. Fetch Aunt Hettie. Tell her I need her help."

He continued trying to force Alex to breathe. He thought that the fluttering pulse responded. Or was it only his desperate imagination?

There was no sign of a bullet wound or a head blow. Only a faint smear of blood at the throat.

Then Jeff found the cause. A rawhide thong was lashed around Alex's throat. It was a saddle string. He had been garroted.

Jeff got out his pocketknife and cut the thong. It had been drawn tight so viciously that it had cut into the flesh and was sticky with Alex's blood. The dry rawhide had stretched a trifle when bloodsoaked—just enough to let life linger tenaciously.

Hettie arrived. She cast off grief and panic. She was now the assistant, impersonal and experienced.

"Larynx damaged, or possibly paralyzed," Jeff said. "Possibly the trachea too. Little air reaching the lungs. I've got to operate right here. He's too far gone to be moved. I'll try a laryngotomy. Fetch the intubation instruments. The ones he calls the O'Dwyer kit. He got one a few years ago during that diphtheria siege."

"Yes," Hettie said, and rushed away.

He continued his attempt to strengthen respiration in Alex. He was not successful.

Hettie returned with the instruments. He swiftly prepared for the operation. He spoke to the Professor and Clem as he worked. "I've never performed a laryngotomy. I'm going to make an incision in the larynx and insert a tube, hoping to get air to his lungs."

He made the incision. A laryngotomy was easier than a full-dress entry into the trachea. And simpler. That, at least, was what the lecturer had said that day in the clinic at the school of anatomy. Not a difficult feat for a trained surgeon, if performed with decision and precision.

Its adverse feature was that the operation was usually necessary under extreme conditions in moments of emergency.

Extreme conditions! The lecturer had meant this particular case. The patient lying on straw in a stable lighted by oil lamps. Gasping for breath. Dying!

And this patient was more than a friend. He was a man who must not die. He was a man who must live.

Jeff completed the incision and placed the tube. He was soaked with perspiration and did not know it. He worked desperately, trying to maintain the flickering pulse of life in Alex, trying by sheer force of will to compel him to live.

He listened. Alex was breathing. The sound in the tube was audible to all of them.

It began to fade.

Jeff said in anguish, "Alex! Alex!"

He fought frantically. But there was no sound from the tube now. No sound at all.

Jeff kept it up, trying with every skill he had been taught to restore life, trying to remember what the lecturer had said that day that seemed so long ago, trying to recall what other lecturers in other clinics had said.

Beside him, Hettie knelt, the tears streaming. She was praying.

"He's got to live!" Jeff panted.

At last he felt the Professor's hand on his shoulder. "It's all over, Jefferson," the Professor said. "There's nothing more you can do."

"There *is!*" Jeff said thickly. "There must be *something!*"

But it *was* ended. His hands finally slackened away from the terrible, hopeless task. He slumped there, utterly spent, looking at Alex's still face. "I couldn't do it, Alex," he said. "I didn't know how to do it. There must have been a way. I'm not a good doctor."

Hettie took him in her arms, drawing his head against her. "No! No! It's the Lord's will. You did everything for him that could be done on earth."

The Professor's hand was still on his shoulder. He finally let the Professor walk him out of the stable and to the house.

He moved blindly. He entered Alex's medical shop. He stood by the operating table and smashed a palm down on its surface in futile agony.

"What was it I did wrong?" he asked harshly. "Why did I have to lose him too? I lost Angie. Now Alex."

It was Clem who answered. "You didn't kill Alex." He added, and his voice was no longer gentle, "But we know who did."

"Yes," Jeff said. "Yes."

He had not even taken the time to remove his gunbelt, so desperate had been the fight for Alex's life, so precious had been the seconds.

"If only we'd found him sooner," he said.

Neighbors had arrived and were taking charge of Hettie, trying to soothe her grief.

Jeff walked out of the house with Clem and the Professor at his side.

"This is my responsibility," he said to them.

"And ours," the Professor answered. "We do not like duplicity. Nor do we like murderers. We're in this with you."

They turned into DeSmet Street and walked to the Stockman's Hotel. Darkness had come. Only a few of the windows in the railroad offices showed light.

They entered the lobby. It was deserted. The hotel owner appeared at a door from the rear. He looked at them and said, "We don't want any more of you Camo people in this place, Temple. I've given orders to Hammond to move his offices out of this hotel inside of forty-eight hours."

"Is Hammond up there?" Jeff asked.

The man gave them a closer look, then backed off a step. "I—I don't know."

Jeff led the way up the stairs. The Camo offices had closed for the day, but two of them were lighted. The door of one stood open, and a cleaning woman was busy inside.

The anteroom of Hammond's office was also lighted, but its door was closed. Jeff tried the knob. The door was locked. He rapped on it with his knuckles.

The voice of Polly, Hammond's secretary, answered. "Who is it?"

"Jeff Temple," Jeff said. "Hammond, are you in there?"

Polly's voice came closer and was shrill. "He's not here."

"Then it's you I want to talk to," Jeff said.

"Go away!"

Jeff backed off and rammed the door with his shoulder. The lock snapped and he staggered in.

Polly was racing to shelter back of her desk. She decided to scream. Jeff crossed the room, grasped her by the arms and sat her down in her chair.

"Never mind giving out with the war whoops," he said. "Where's Hammond?"

"Leave me alone!" she gasped. She stared, terrified, at Jeff's companions as they entered the office.

The Professor made one of his sweeping bows. "Ephraim Kelso, Miss. At your service. This is Clement Devore. You apparently have already met my good friend, Jefferson Temple."

"I know who you are," Polly said shakily. "Please go away."

The Professor replaced his hat, beaming. "Now, if you will be so kind as to apprise us of the whereabouts of Mr. Hammond, we will be in your debt indeed."

"What do you want with him?"

Jeff answered that. "We have one or two matters to take up with him. Such as murder, maybe."

Polly suddenly lost her brassy front. "I had nothing to do with—with—"

"With what?"

"With—with anything."

"Where's Hammond?"

"I haven't seen him in—in some time."

"Then you've had word from him," Jeff said. "Where is he?"

She swallowed hard. She tried to face it out but didn't have the courage. "He's—he's sick. He's in his car. His private car in the railroad yards."

Jeff stood looking at her. "You do know about this, don't you," he said. "All about it, most likely."

They left the room. The cleaning woman was still busy in the adjoining offices as they passed down the hall.

Jeff suddenly halted in stride. "Wait a minute!"

He returned to the open door of the room in which the woman was busy. She was middle-aged, marked by a patient life of drudgery.

Jeff removed his hat. "You're from the settlers' camp, I take it, ma'am?" he asked.

"Yes I am, Mr. Temple," she said.

"So you know me."

"I saw you there the night of the shootin'."

"There were two of you ladies working here that night before the shooting started," Jeff said. "Where's the other lady?"

"That was my sister," the woman said. "Poor Jennie. Poor, poor Jennie. She's dead. She's the one they killed."

"Jennie Barnes!" Jeff was speaking more to himself than to the Professor and Clem. "So that's how it was. I saw her face that night as she lay dead. There's a lot of family resemblance between you. It struck me just now as I passed by the door."

"I'm Hannah Larson," the woman said. "I had come here to help Jennie that night, for she wanted to get through early so she could get back to the camp an' enjoy the music an' the dancin'. She'd be alive now if I hadn't helped her."

She was weeping. "Mr. Hammond gave me the work here. It earns us a little money. Mr. Hammond's a kind man."

Clem repeated it. "Hammond's a kind man."

The three of them left the hotel. "He's a very kind man," Jeff said.

They walked down DeSmet Street into Hammond Street. A few faces came to the doors to stare after them as they passed by. They crossed the street and entered the Camo railroad yards.

They located Bill Hammond's private palace car on a sidetrack, dismally surrounded by boxcars and empty cattle cars. The velvet curtains were tightly drawn but there was light within.

The vestibule stood open but it was dark and deserted. The door leading into the car was closed and curtained. The three of them ascended the steps into the vestibule.

Jeff tried the handle of the door. It opened and he stepped into the lighted interior. The Professor and Clem remained in the vestibule, with the toe of Clem's boot holding the door slightly ajar.

There were half a dozen men in the car, but Jeff's quiet

entrance went unnoticed for a moment or two. The air was hazed with tobacco smoke. Liquor bottles and glasses stood on tables handy to the occupants. A porter in a white jacket moved among them with a tray. The car was equipped with red plush armchairs and settees. Thick carpet gave queasy underfooting. Gas mantles, nestled among crystal chandeliers, lighted the car. The galley and sleeping quarters occupied compartments.

Bill Hammond sat in a big armchair, poring over papers that were scattered on a low table before him. He had a cigar clenched in his strong teeth. He wore a loose smoking jacket and a soft white shirt open at the throat without a necktie. His feet were in boots of soft leather that were well made but of a conventional black finish. A pistol was in a holster that he had hung on the back of a chair nearby.

Three of the men were playing stud poker at a table, with money in sight. One was Arch Stanton. Another was Fletcher Jones, who was studying his opponent's hands with squinting, calculating eyes. The third player was a swarthy man whose name Jeff did not know. Bass Brackett, burly and saturnine, sat dozing in a chair, a quart bottle of beer within reach.

All were armed. Arch Stanton was packing double. The tips of his weighted holsters hung down on either side of his chair.

It was Stanton who first became aware of Jeff's presence. He looked up and spent a moment of careful appraisal. He spoke softly. "Look who's here, Bill."

# CHAPTER FIFTEEN

Hammond swung around and gazed. He laid aside the papers. "Jeff! It's high time we were hearing from you!"

Jeff looked at Arch Stanton. "I figured I'd find you here, Arch."

Stanton smiled. "It's been this way all along. Even at the church we were there to back you up."

"And nobody was backing the ranchers?" Jeff asked.

"That's right," Stanton said. "You didn't understand."

"I do now," Jeff said.

Hammond spoke jovially. "Pour yourself a drink, Jeff. Where in blazes have you been?"

The card game had halted. Stanton hitched around in his chair and sat apparently relaxed, his arms dangling.

"I went hunting," Jeff said. "Down in the Hills."

"How did you do?" Hammond asked.

"Very good," Jeff said. "I bagged some big game."

"How was that?"

"I was called to the Mackay ranch. Peter Mackay had a bullet in his arm. He was in bad shape. He'd neglected it. It was close to gangrene. It was his left arm."

Hammond slapped a palm down on the table. "Now what do you know about that? You *did* bag something big, Jeff. I was sure from the start it was Pete who had ramrodded those fools when they shot up the Zulus. This proves it. Now why would a man go that loco?"

"Mackay tells a wild story about men slugging him at his ranch hours after the Zulu shooting," Jeff said. "He told me that when he came out of it he found that he had the bullet in his arm."

Hammond stared incredulously, then laughed. "Does he expect anybody to believe that?"

The others laughed too. Except Arch Stanton. His face remained unreadable as he watched Jeff.

"I didn't believe it either," Jeff said. He added, "At first."

Hammond's amiable smile remained, but it was now only fixed there. Like a mask. "Ramon Montez is out of jail, Jeff," he said. "He was turned loose late this afternoon. I saw to it. Camo has withdrawn all charges against him."

"You're a man of your word, Bill," Jeff said.

"I am," Hammond said. "I've carried out my part of our agreement."

"And the same here," Jeff said. "I'm seeing to it that the Zulus get a fair deal. That was the agreement. I've still got a couple of matters to wind up. There's the murder of Jennie Barnes, for instance. And Ralph Slocum."

"Jeff," Hammond said chidingly, "you seem to be driving at something. Something I don't like."

"What's on Peter Mackay's ranch—or under it—that you're after?" Jeff asked.

"Now what does that have to do with protecting the Zulus?" Hammond asked.

Arch Stanton turned his head and eyed Hammond coldly. "I always had a hunch there was more in this than that bunch of sagebrush and a few damned cattle, Bill. And I agreed to work for you for a few measly hundred a month."

Hammond shrugged. "You'll find it worthwhile. You and everybody here. That goes for you too, Jeff."

"That's nice," Jeff said. "Up until today I wasn't sure which side anybody was on. Now I know. We're all pulling together. For you, Bill. Those fifty-dollar bills all came from one bankroll. Yours."

"That's right," Hammond said.

"You were running both ends of this war," Jeff went on. "It wasn't cattlemen who raided the Zulu camp. Nor was it Zulus who hit the Mackay place. It was the same bunch both times. Arch Stanton, or his men."

"You're smart, Jeff," Hammond said ironically.

"And you always were pretty smart yourself at running a high blaze," Jeff said.

The Professor and Clem now decided to make their presence known. They entered the car and stood at Jeff's elbow. The porter, who had been listening with growing fright, now fled to the safety of his galley.

"Adroit is the proper term for Mr. Hammond," the Professor said. "Or cunning. But not smart. Murder is never smart."

"But you're a good judge of human nature, at least, Bill," Jeff said. "You knew how to prod Teddy Roosevelt into handing you what you wanted."

"You flatter me," Hammond said. "So I influence presidents?"

"Roosevelt is a man who takes the side of the underdog," Jeff said. "The cattlemen are in the right, but they've been made to look like thugs and murderers with this fake war that you and Stanton engineered. I'm sure you've seen to it that the White House has heard all about what rascals the ranchers are."

"They *are* rascals," Hammond said mockingly. "Otherwise I wouldn't have needed your help, Jeff."

The Professor uttered a snort of derision. "What you wanted was to have the name of Temple connected with your scheme. I am personally aware of the President's high regard for Jefferson's father."

"What was it that caused Jennie Barnes to recognize you as you helped shoot up the Zulus?" Jeff asked.

Hammond stopped pretending to be amused. "Quit this hoorawing," he said.

"It was something that Ralph Slocum noticed too," Jeff said.

"You're beginning to bore me, Jeff."

Jeff looked at Hammond's boots and had an inspiration. "What became of the hundred-dollar bench-mades, Bill?" he asked. "The ones of alligator leather?"

He saw that he had touched on a sensitive nerve. He nodded. "I guessed it, didn't I?"

"Keep guessing," Hammond snapped.

"A man always seems to overlook something," Jeff said. "You shouldn't have worn those fancy boots that night, Bill. You saw that your cleaning woman had spotted them while you were helping shoot up the Zulu camp. A potato-sack mask and a slicker wasn't enough. You were supposed to be the Zulus' friend and protector. If they had found out that you were also posing as a cattleman as well as trying to win the President's sympathy for the Zulus, the cat would be out of the bag. You made sure Jennie Barnes didn't talk."

Some of the color had left Hammond's face. There was the hint of panic in his eyes.

"You must have shot her before you considered the consequences, Bill," Jeff went on. "After going in that deep you had to murder Ralph Slocum so he wouldn't talk either."

"You know *you're* talking too much too, don't you, Jeff?" Hammond rasped.

"A lot of people heard Slocum say he could identify the man who killed Jennie Barnes," Jeff said. "He must have seen the boots too. So you had to get rid of him, and in a hurry."

He looked at Stanton. "Or maybe it was you who picked Slocum off, Arch. Or Brackett, or Fletch Jones there."

Stanton waved that aside indifferently. "What I'm interested in, is what you've found out there in the Hills, Bill. Is it gold?"

Hammond merely broke an ash from his cigar and did not answer.

"Why did you ride on that raid, Bill?" Jeff asked. "It was a risk."

When Hammond still didn't speak, Jeff answered the question himself. "My guess is that you had to prove that you meant business. Arch has dealt with men like you before. He didn't intend to be left holding the bag. So he insisted that you show good faith by joining that raid on the Zulus. He wanted to make sure you were tarred with the same brush. He sent Tass Verity up to the Camo offices that night to tell you to come along with them—or else. I saw Tass there."

Arch Stanton's lips carried the ghost of a smile. Ham- again hitting close to the truth.

"You were so mad at being whipsawed into it that you forgot about those alligator boots," he continued. "You must have left your office right after I had talked to you that night."

Arch Stanton spoke. "Maybe you can tell me what Hammond's after out there in the Hills, Temple?"

"Whatever it is, his uncle, Tass Verity, got onto it two or three years ago," Jeff said. "He core-drilled until he had proved out where the stuff lies. Apparently it's on Peter Mackay's patented land. Tass kept it quiet until he could figure out an airtight way to get his hands on Mackay's ranch. He went to you. Between you, this railroad scheme was thought up. Tass probably put up the money to get it started, and stock was sold to pay the rest of it."

"This still isn't telling us what's down there," Stanton said impatiently.

"I think it's copper," Jeff said. "That's it, isn't it, Bill?"

Stanton slapped his knee. "Why, sure! This country reminds me a lot of that damned desert down on the Arizona border where they hit copper rich. How about *that,* Bill?"

Hammond was driven into a corner. "All right," he snarled. "It's copper. But it's low-grade. An open pit job. It'll take money to develop it."

"And it's on the Mackay ranch?" Stanton asked.

"The best of it. That damned Mackay ranch house is sitting right in the middle of it."

"How deep down?" Jeff asked.

"That's my business," Hammond growled.

"Why did you have Camo drill just off the edge of Mackay's fence line only last year?"

"I wanted to make sure Tass wasn't running a sandy on me," Hammond said. "He wasn't lying. It's there. Copper."

The Professor spoke. "Honor among thieves. Mr. Hammond didn't even trust his own kin. This also explains why that Verity rascal pilfered that length of rock core that was lying around the Mackay place. He didn't want anyone to become curious and have it assayed."

"You never intended for Camo to be built any farther than the Walking Hills, did you, Bill?" Jeff spoke. "You knew that Zulus would force Peter Mackay to move out of the country, and it wouldn't be much of a trick to have him sell his land for what you might want to offer. It wouldn't be long before the Zulus would be starved out. Maybe by that time even what stockholders there were who had bought into Camo would be frozen out. You'd have not only a copper mine, but you'd even have a railroad already built to haul it to market."

"You'll be well taken care of," Hammond snapped.

"It was Brackett, here, who led the bunch that shot up the Mackay ranch last night," Jeff said. "I take it that you were in on it too, Fletch, and your sidekick there. That was done to prod the cattlemen into really going after the Zulus. But none of you boys intended to be around when the shooting started."

"You can't prove any of this stuff," Hammond said.

"Let's see your left arm, Bill," Jeff said.

That brought a moment of silence. Arch Stanton spoke. "Where do you stand in this, Temple?"

"Right here looking at you," Jeff said.

"There are five of us," Stanton said. "Three of you."

A new voice spoke. "Four is the correct number, senor."

Jeff, without turning his attention from the men he was facing, knew who had stepped into the car back of him.

"I heard they'd let you go, Ramon," he said. "Pull out of here. This is no place for you. You're a married man, with a family."

"I will stay," Ramon said. He was a sinewy, dashingly-handsome man with a skin like bronze. He wore a leather vest cut in the gaucho style and had a sash around his waist. Otherwise his garb was that of his adopted land—weather-faded denims and flannel shirt and half boots. He had a six-shooter in his sash.

"Dolores is waiting for you," Jeff said. "And the little ones."

"It was Dolores who told me to find you," Ramon said. "I have done that."

"Welcome to the party, amigo," the Professor said.

Jeff spoke to Bill Hammond. "I asked about your arm, Bill. Your left arm. How's it coming along?"

"There's nothing wrong with my arm," Hammond said.

"You went into hiding after Slocum put that bullet in your arm, Bill," Jeff said. "Stanton stayed with you. You knew you stood a good chance of being lynched if anyone found out about that puncture. So you sent Stanton to try to put the guilt on Peter Mackay. Or maybe it was your uncle, Tass Verity, who thought up the idea. One or the other of them trailed Mackay when he left Wardrum that night. Both of them, probably. They waylaid him at his own ranch before daybreak."

"You still can't prove any of this," Hammond said.

"The proof's there under that jacket," Jeff said. "You made the same mistake Mackay made. He was innocent but he knew the odds were against him. He tried to doctor his arm himself. So did you. But it didn't work. By last night you knew you had to have professional help or die. So you went to Alex Crabtree's house. Nobody else was there. You made sure of that. Aunt Hettie was at prayer meeting. The Professor and Clem were uptown."

"I should have known you'd turn against me, Jeff," Hammond said.

Jeff nodded. "You also must have known that I wouldn't stand for what happened to Jennie Barnes and Ralph Slocum."

He drew from his pocket the bullet he had found in Alex Crabtree's office. He tossed it, but Hammond made no attempt to catch it. The slug landed in the thick carpet.

"Or to Alex Crabtree," Jeff said. "Alex Crabtree, above all."

He looked at Arch Stanton. "I'm sure you were in on that, Stanton. Are you the one who pulled that slipknot tight around Alex's neck after you had forced him to take that bullet out of Hammond's arm?"

It was Stanton who could no longer stand the tension. He rolled from his chair, drawing and firing at Jeff.

Jeff's counter-move was equally swift. He twisted aside, his pistol rising into his hand and roaring.

Both slugs missed because both men were moving. Jeff fired again. Stanton's gun also blazed a second time but it was Jeff who scored. Stanton was shaken by the impact of a slug. He tried instinctively to bring his pistol to bear again, but his strength failed him.

The solid roar of gunfire jarred the car. Every man was shooting. The Professor was crouched back of an overturned table, using a .45 with his right hand, holding a second pistol in reserve in his left hand.

Clem had dropped flat on the carpet. Ramon Montez had overturned an armchair and knelt back of it as he fired.

The mantles of the gas lamps were broken by the explosions. A few wavering tongues of pale flame survived. These flickered and recoiled amid the sheet lightning of the gunfire.

The first fury of the battle broke off. Silence came. Jeff

crouched, waiting, peering through the fog of powder fumes. The flames of the gas tapers steadied.

Arch Stanton was not dead. He tenaciously lifted a pistol and fired. Jeff felt the bullet burn along his rib in a fiery graze. That shot had been intended for his heart.

He brought his gun to bear on Stanton but did not shoot, for Stanton had slumped down on his face, the piston falling from his fingers.

Clem's two pistols exploded. Bass Brackett, down the car, said in a shocked, moaning voice, "God! Don't shoot ag'in. I've—" His voice dribbled off. His bubbling breathing faded and stopped.

Fletcher Jones sat on the floor, looking dazedly at a bullet-broken leg that lay bent grotesquely beneath him. The shock of his wound had numbed him.

The fifth man, who lay flat on the floor, shouted, "I'm out of this. I didn't fire a shot. I didn't hire out to fight you fellas."

"All right," Jeff said. "So you're out of it. See that you stay out of it."

The Professor was still crouched nearby. Clem and Ramon were unhurt. They were flattened back of furniture, reloading.

Jeff said, "Hammond?"

Bill Hammond did not answer. But he was there. And alive. Jeff could hear him breathing back of the heavy armchair where he had taken refuge when the fight had started. He had done some shooting, but he had not offered himself as a target.

"Come out, Bill," Jeff said. "You're the only one left."

Hammond did not answer.

Jeff looked at the Professor. "Are you all right?" he exclaimed.

The Professor was leaning against an overturned chair. Jeff touched him. The Professor looked at him and said, "Good-by, Jefferson. It was a privilege to know men like you and Clement."

"Professor!" Jeff exclaimed protestingly.

Clem came to the Professor's side. "Ephraim!"

"No regrets," the Professor murmured. "No regrets!"

He leaned his head against Jeff's shoulder. His frock coat was soaked with crimson dampness.

Jeff tore open the coat and ripped the shirt, trying to locate the wound. "Wait!" he said frantically. "Wait! I'll help you—"

The Professor sagged against him. He was smiling faintly—his old tolerant, half-cynical smile. There was no waiting for him.

Presently Jeff lowered the Professor's body to the floor and folded his hands across his chest. He and Clem looked at each other. Ramon made the sign of the cross.

"He wasn't born to be a professor," Clem said. "He wanted to be with people like us. This is the way he wanted to go. No, he had no regrets."

Jeff could hear a horse galloping over the ties and gravel of the tracks. Its rider halted near the car, dismounted and came racing up the steps. "Jeff! Jeff Temple!"

The arrival was Lila. "Mr. Devore!" she continued to call frantically. "Ramon! Mr. Kelso!"

The tightness became intolerable in Jeff's throat. Mr. Kelso was the only one who would never be able to answer.

Lila pushed open the door. Her face was chalk-white. Her eyes fixed on Jeff. Then she came to him with a rush. Wild thankfulness was in her face. She put her arms around him, uttering little choked sounds. "I had given you up for dead," she sobbed.

She now saw the Professor. And she wept for him.

Jeff motioned to Ramon. "Take her away," he said. "Take her to Dolores."

For there was still Bill Hammond to deal with. But Lila clung to him, not understanding. And Hammond saw his chance. He had Jeff at a disadvantage. He thrust an arm above his barricade, aiming a six-shooter.

Jeff was in no position to fire. He twisted around in order to shield Lila. It was Clem who saved him. Clem fired before Hammond's weapon exploded. The bullet spun Hammond around and he pitched to the floor. His wild shot brought down a cascade of broken crystals from the chandelier.

Jeff moved to his side. The slug had ripped upward along Hammond's right arm. It was an ugly, flesh-shattering wound. Blood was spurting with each throb of Hammond's heart.

Hammond was conscious. The shock of the injury numbed the pain. Jeff, with Clem's help, stripped off Hammond's smoking jacket and tore away his shirt.

They looked at each other. Hammond's left arm bore a bandage. A neat, professional bandage. Alex Crabtree's handiwork.

Jeff clamped his fingers around Hammond's arm above the wound, checking the loss of blood. He said to Clem,

"Take my place until I can get a tourniquet formed. Clamp your fingers where I have mine. Grab hard. As hard as you can. Block the flow of blood."

Hammond tried to wrest his arm free of Jeff's grasp. "Let it go, Jeff," he murmured. "Let it flow. That'll be the easiest way. You know what I'm in for if I live."

"Grip that arm, Clem," Jeff said.

Clem did not move. "Let him die," he said harshly. He turned and looked at the Professor's still face. "Let him die," he repeated.

Jeff shook his head. "You know you can't do that. We're not the ones to decide things like that."

"Your Hippocratic oath?" Clem demanded.

"No, Clem. It's just the way we are. We're not killers."

Clem did not move for a bitter moment. Then the bleakness softened, the savagery faded. "Yes," he finally said. "Yes."

He closed his fingers on Hammond's arm, following Jeff's directions. Again Hammond tried to fend them off, but did not have the strength and finally lay back, closing his eyes.

"Damn both of you and your consciences," he gasped.

With the spurt of blood effectively checked, Jeff formed a bandage from strips torn from garments that permitted loosening of the tourniquet.

He did what he could for Fletcher Jones, who lay stupefied by the pain of his bullet-shattered leg.

"That'll take care of them both until they can be got to an operating table," he said. "They need considerably more attention."

Bass Brackett was dead, as was Arch Stanton. Ramon had disarmed the gunman who had surrendered and had him standing facing a wall.

Lila laid a hand on Jeff's arm. "The cattlemen are on their way to Wardrum," she said. "I saw them leave the Block T just before dark. I rode fast and got here ahead of them, but they can't be far away now. Aunt Hettie told me you and Clem and the Professor had gone somewhere in town. Then I heard the shooting, so I came here."

The shooting had also brought others from town. One of the arrivals was Sheriff Lish Carter.

Jeff pointed to the wounded men. "They're your responsibility now, Lish," he said. "Send someone to get one of the other doctors. Or both of them. Alex Crabtree is dead. Murdered. I'll tell you about it later. I've got other business to take care of."

The deep rumble of hoofs was rising in the town. Many horses.

Jeff left the car. Clem and Ramon moved with him. Lila also stayed at his side. He started to order her back to the car, but she linked her arm tightly in his. "This is where I belong," she said.

She added. "You're hurt, you know. There's blood on your side."

"It's only a graze," he said. "It's nothing. It can wait." He eyed her, grinning. "And that's a professional opinion. I can promise you that if there's one time in my life I don't want to turn up my toes, it's now. And you know why."

"Maybe," she said. "But I'd rather have you tell me."

"At the right time and place," he said. "Which, I hope, will be soon."

They ran down the tracks until they came in sight of the Zulu camp. It was a bristling fortress. The Zulus had barricaded and were crouched there, armed with the rifles that Bill Hammond had furnished them.

Jeff lifted his voice. "There'll be no fighting. This has all been a frame-up on the part of Camo and Bill Hammond."

The roar of hoofs was near at hand. Jeff and his companions turned and crossed the Camo tracks and walked to the corner of Hammond and DeSmet Streets.

DeSmet Street was black with the mass of oncoming cattlemen. There must have been more than forty of them, the total fighting strength of Walking Hills. And in their midst rode Tass Verity, shouting and beating the drums of hatred.

Jeff and his companions halted abreast in the center of the street, and the cattlemen drew up.

"There's going to be no war!" Jeff shouted. "There never was one. You've been bamboozled, double-crossed."

Tass Verity rose in the stirrups, glaring. "Git out of the way, Temple!" he roared. But there was fear in him. He was of a mind to draw, but his courage failed him.

"Don't let Tass get away," Jeff said. "You there, Dan Mulhall. And you, Evans Johnson. See to it that Tass doesn't make a break for it. Bill Hammond has committed murders, and Tass was in on it. The truth has come out."

He began telling it. He had barely uttered a dozen words before Verity drove spurs to his horse and tried to break away through the surrounding press of riders. But men seized the reins of his horse and halted him, forcing him to sit there.

Jeff walked to his side and dragged him from the saddle. The Zulus had now left their barricades to come swarming across the tracks in order to listen.

Jeff singled out Tom Carstairs. He dragged Tass Verity bodily for a dozen yards and sent him spinning at Carstairs' feet. "Here's the chance to pay off for being tarred, Carstairs," he said. "That was done, too, on orders of either Verity or his nephew. After you're through with him, hand him over to Lish Carter."

While both Zulus and cattlemen listened, he told the whole story of how they had been used as dupes in an attempt to sway a president.

And Bill Hammond's scheme had succeeded in that respect, at least. Even before Jeff was finished talking, a wild-eyed man came running from the telegraph office in the railroad depot. He was the Western Union operator.

"Teddy Roosevelt's signed the charter," the operator screeched. "Camo's got the land grant. He's signed the bill to open the Hills. It'll be a law in thirty days."

The man looked around at the silent faces. "What's the matter with you people?" he demanded. "Didn't you hear? This is what you Zulus has been waitin' for, ain't it? What are you jest standin' there for? Ain't you goin' to celebrate?"

"Of course you're going to celebrate!" Jeff shouted. "Don't you understand? There's copper down there. You won't have to starve on a dry farm. Even if you don't hit on any part of the ore when you file, you'll have plenty of jobs with good pay. This country is going to boom. It'll be both cattle and copper from now on. There's big money to be made."

They aroused. A murmur went up that grew to a roar. Zulus began to race back to camp to carry the news to their families. The weapons in their hands were only burdens now.

Afterward, Jeff and Lila returned to the Crabtree house. Clem and Ramon accompanied them. Hammond and Fletcher Jones were being worked on by the other two doctors. There had been talk of lynching, but Jeff had silenced that.

The Professor and Alex lay beneath sheets in the back room at Ozzie Stone's furniture store, along with the bodies of Arch Stanton and Bass Brackett. Lila had lighted tall candles over all of them. It seemed appropriate, even though the religions of none of them were known. There could be no feuds in death.

Hettie was sad, but composed. She kissed Jeff. Lila took her in her arms.

Jeff walked into Alex's medical shop and stood there remembering many things. Presently Lila joined him. They were silent, neither wanting to put into words the thoughts of the moment.

Jeff listened to the approach of a fast-moving horse and the creak of a rattletrap vehicle. He had heard this same sound not too long in the past. It halted before the house. Footsteps thudded on the porch.

"Doc!" an excited man shouted as he pounded on the screen door. "Doc Crabb! It's fer sure this time. The baby! It's on its way. Hurry! Hurry!"

The arrival was Henry, the same young expectant father who had once before called Alex away. Hettie admitted him. He looked around anxiously. "Where's the doctor?" he asked.

Jeff saw that Lila was watching him. She was smiling a little as though she was in on some secret.

Jeff stood gazing at her. He moved toward her and she came to meet him, still smiling. "How proud I am of you," she said.

He took her in his arms and kissed her. She clung to him. She was still trying to smile, but now she was weeping.

At last he reluctantly released her. He looked at the expectant father. "I hope this isn't another false alarm, Henry," he said. "I was here the other day when you came."

"Are you a doctor?" the man asked.

It was Lila who answered. "Yes. He's a doctor."

She linked arms with Jeff. "I'm going along," she said. "I might be able to help."

"Are you sure?" he asked.

"Sure of what?"

"That you want to be a doctor's wife."

She gave him one of her slanting looks. "Very sure," she said. She added, "Doctor."

Aunt Hettie had found Alex's medical bag. She handed it to him, and he and Lila followed Henry out of the house and to the waiting vehicle.

**Cliff Farrell** was born in Zanesville, Ohio, where earlier Zane Grey had been born. Following graduation from high school, Farrell became a newspaper reporter. Over the next decade he worked his way west by means of a string of newspaper jobs and for thirty-one years was employed, mostly as sports editor, for the *Los Angeles Examiner*. He would later claim that he began writing for pulp magazines because he grew bored with journalism. His first Western stories were written for *Cowboy Stories* in 1926 and his byline was A. Clifford Farrell. By 1928 this byline was abbreviated to Cliff Farrell, and this it remained for the rest of his career. In 1933 Farrell was invited to contribute a story for the first issue of *Dime Western*. He soon became a regular contributor to this magazine and to *Star Western* as well. In fact, many months he would have a short novel in both magazines. Farrell became such a staple at Popular Publications that by the end of the 1930s he was contributing as much as 400,000 words a year to their various Western magazines. In all, Farrell wrote nearly 600 stories for the magazine market. His earliest Western fiction tended to stress action and gun play, but increasingly his stories began to focus on characters in historical situations and the problems faced by those characters. *Follow the New Grass* (1954) was Farrell's first Western novel, a story concerned with a desperate battle over the grazing rights in the Cheyenne Indian reserve. It was followed by *West with the Missouri* (1955), an exciting story of riverboats, gamblers, and gunmen. *Fort Deception* (1960), *Ride The Wild Country* (1963), *The Renegade* (1970), and *The Devil's Playground* (1976) are among the best of Farrell's later Western novels. *Desperate Journey*, a first collection of Cliff Farrell's Western short stories, will soon be appearing as a Five Star Western.